Obsidian

Other books by David J Hawkes:

The Tarnished Angel
Shoshone Trail
Shoshone Trail II: Hans' Pass

Obsidian

David J Hawkes

Council Press
Springville, Utah

ISBN: 1-55517-859-6
v.1

Published by Council Press,
an imprint of Cedar Fort, Inc.
925 N. Main Springville, Utah., 84663
www.cedarfort.com

Distributed by:

Cover design by Nicole Williams
Cover design © 2005 by Lyle Mortimer

Printed in the United States of America
10 9 8 7 6 5 4 3 2 1

Printed on acid-free paper

dedication

To Susan, my best friend

Prologue

It had taken the old man longer than usual to make the hike into the high mountain basin this year. Stopping to wipe at the thin film of sweat that had formed on his forehead, he pushed back the battered grey Stetson and let his eyes take in the view. It was as it always had been. Several rivers of golden-leaved aspen flowed downward through the dark green of the fir timber and in the bottom of the shallow basin, a sparkling stream wound its way through the willow-lined banks. Breathing deeply of the mountain air, a smile broke out on the old man's face. It was good to be back.

With a small pack on his back, he gripped his polished maple staff and walked a few yards farther over the sage-covered ridge and down into the basin. His eyes searching out the small basin, he looked for any sign of elk. Nothing. But then he wasn't carrying a rifle anyway. He hadn't for four years now.

Ever since Rachel's passing.

But still he came.

It was as if every year at this time he was drawn to this place. This place was as a magnet to his soul. A place of healing and of remembering.

Chuckling a little to himself, he had almost had to sneak away this year. At ninety years old, he had no one living with him, but the neighbors being as they were, tried to keep an eye on him. Dennis, his nearest neighbor, had stopped by several days before and hinted he would take him elk hunting this year, but he couldn't take opening day off so it would have to be on the weekend. And Len, another of his neighbors, had warned him about going alone but he had got up well before daylight and driven his pickup as far as he could on the rutted mountain road before beginning his hike.

A cool breeze brushed his face and carried with it the smells of early fall. The aspen and fir, the dampness of last evenings shower, and the pungent odor of the elk.

Yes they were here.

Somewhere.

Just a few feet further down the low ridge, the old man could see the battered trunk of a single, slender lodgepole pine that had been assaulted by a bull elk. The lower branches tattered and broken with the bark peeled off, gave the tree the appearance of having been worked on no more than a few hours before. Taking the few steps to the solitary tree, the old man touched the wet sap with a forefinger. *Not long ago,* he thought to himself. Then from further down in the basin he heard the thin, high pitch of the bull as he bugled. He felt the goose bumps rise along his arms. The sound of a bull's bugle never failed, even after all the years, to bring chills to his very core. From a pocket of his faded red shirt he took a small pair of binoculars and put them to his eyes. For several minutes he searched the small basin, but nowhere could he see the elk. Patience, he thought to himself.

Not until the morning sun began to touch the western ridges did the old man notice movement in the aspen along the bottom of the basin. Focusing the binoculars on the movement he could see the tan and brown forms of elk. First several cows and calves, then another cow, and finally bringing up the rear, the bull.

Ivory-tipped antlers swept over his back, the bull trotted into the opening between the aspen and the willow-lined stream. Steam lifting from his back, the bull bugled again.

From his spot near the beaten pine the old man smiled and with an exaggerated gesture doffed his weather-stained Stetson. Seeing the movement, the lead cow stared hard at the old man then with a sharp bark of alarm bolted for the timber on the far side of the stream. Watching the small bunch of elk splash through the water and thunder into the timber, he smiled. Yes, it was still a thrill.

"Magnificent," he softly whispered.

After the elk had disappeared, the old man watched the sunlight creep down the far ridge toward the bottom of the basin. Working the small pack onto his thin shoulders, he looked for a spot to sit. There was a likely place, a rounded white boulder that gave him a complete view of the basin. Making his way to the boulder, he stopped once to catch his breath. How many more years would he be able to make this trek he wondered? No matter he mused, he had made it again this year.

Reaching the rock, he walked along the side of it until he came to spot that was shaped almost like a chair. Pulling his pack off, he set it on the ground and then slid onto the smooth surface of the boulder. Perfect! Then for a moment he wondered why he had never seen this particular boulder before? He had ridden his horse or walked into this very basin at least a hundred times in his life. Surely, he would have seen this one sometime? Dismissing the thought, the old man reached for his pack and noticed on the ground, half covered with dirt a smooth black object. Sliding from his perch, he dug around the edges with his fingers. It turned out to be a long partially chipped piece of obsidian. Turning the glass-like stone in his hand, it was obvious to the old man it had been intended as a spear or lance point. Once again he reached for his pack but not for one of the candy bars. This time he took out a leather glove and a small, antler tine taken from a Mule Deer he had killed more than fifty years before. Putting the leather glove on his left hand, he took the piece of obsidian and with the antler tine in his right, flaked a few chips from the partially made lance point. There, the shape was coming. Holding the obsidian at arm's length he looked at the glassy stone carefully. Yes, it wouldn't take but a few more minutes and it would be done. Then pausing for a moment, the old man wondered who it was that had begun the point? Why had he stopped? What had he been like? From the looks of the point it was obvious he had been a craftsman. The flakes that had been chipped from the stone were small, mere particles. Lost in thought, the old man chipped away a few more flakes. A gentle smile on his face, he thought back over the years of his life. He remembered the times he had found ancient arrowheads or spear points. Letting his mind wander as he worked, he thought back to the first.

One

"Did too!"

"Did not! You're just making it up!"

His jaw jutting forward, eight-year-old Bill stared hard at the three older boys. "Did too! My pa says so!"

"Aw, yer pa is as full of it as you are," sneered Bert, the oldest and biggest of the boys.

Angry that the boys would doubt his father's word, Bill took a step toward them. "My pa wouldn't ever lie about nothin'. And besides he's shown me flint chips he's found from down there."

Taking a step closer to Bill, Bert pushed the younger boy. "An' I say your pa is a liar!"

Filled with rage, Bill swung his fist at the bully's face.

A howl of pain escaped Bert, as Bill's fist bloodied his nose, but knowing the fight was on he swung a roundhouse at Bill. Rolling in the dusty lot outside of the wood-frame general store that served the small town, the two boys threw punches and did their best to make the other give in. Then seeing their larger companion was getting the worst of it, Bert's two friends joined in. Within a matter of a few seconds Bill was covering his head and trying his best to ride out the blows and kicks coming from all three boys. Then it stopped.

A rough hand helped him stand and began to wipe the dirt and grass from his overalls and torn shirt.

"What's all the fuss about?" It was the sad eyes and the walrus mustache of Mr. Vereen the storekeeper.

His eyes filled with tears and holding his sides where a particularly vicious kick had caught him, Bill replied, "I tolt them guys that my pa says that the Indians used to camp down by our crick in the pioneer days, and they said Pa was a liar."

"Ah well, them three ain't got any sense anyway," Mr. Vereen grumbled. "Now come on, I'll get you cleaned up."

Dabbing at a cut on his cheek and doing his best to hold his shirt together, Bill followed the older man into the cool confines of the store.

Taking a seat on a wooden chair next to the now cold coal stove that occupied the center of the store, Bill let Mr. Vereen wipe gently at the cut and other scrapes that seemed to cover his face.

"You were holdin' your own purty good until them other two joined in."

"Yes sir," replied Bill. Then watching as the older man began to stitch up the tear in his cotton shirt, he asked hopefully, "You believe me don't you?"

"About what?"

"About the Indians."

"Yup."

"Then why don't Bert and them other guys?"

Tying off the thread and putting the needle and roll of thread away, Mr. Vereen smiled through his mustache, "Ask your pa that question and I reckon you'll git the same answer. Some folks are jist jealous of anything another feller has. Now go on. Get to home and give your pa a hand with the chores."

Still sucking on the peppermint stick the storekeeper had given him, Bill turned up the dusty lane that led to his home. There across the field he could see his father standing with a shovel irrigating the field of alfalfa. Taking a straight route to his father through the field, Bill took in the smells of the wet earth. Nearing his father, he stooped and removed his shoes as he was seeing the flood of water reaching out through the knee high alfalfa. Walking along the wet dirt of the ditch, Bill watched as his father pulled out a canvas dam allowing the water to flow further down the ditch.

"Bill," his father said quietly.

"Hey, Pa," Bill replied.

For a moment neither of them said anything. Then Bill's father asked, "Mind telling me what happened?"

Knowing his father could see the effects of the fight, Bill shrugged his shoulders, "Aw, nothin' much, just Bert being a bully again."

His mind wandering back to his own youth, the corners of his father's mouth turned up, "What about this time?"

Embarrassed, Bill shrugged his shoulders again and

looked down at the swirling brown water.

Then feeling his fathers grey eyes on him, Bill looked up. "Bert said you were a liar."

Seeing the anguish in his son's eyes, Bill's father stepped across the ditch and put his hand on Bill's shoulder. "About what?"

His head held low, Bill replied, "Well you know you been tellin' me about how the Indians used to camp down along the crick back in the olden days."

His father nodded so Bill continued, "I told them guys about it and they said I was full of it and you were just makin' it up."

"Do you think I made it up?"

Looking at his father with tears in his eyes, Bill shook his head, "No."

Staring out across the fields, Bill's father let a grin play across his face. Then sticking the shovel into the mud of the ditch bank he said, "Come on, let's go for a walk."

Following his father, Bill tried to match his fathers long strides with those of his own. Soon they came to the pole fence that separated the alfalfa field from the grassy pasture where they grazed their cattle. Stopping there, Bill's father swung his arm. "Look at it."

For several seconds Bill looked down along the grassy meadow and toward the cottonwood and brush-lined stream. Not knowing if he was seeing what his father was pointing out, he looked up at him.

"You're not sure what I'm seeing are you?" Bill's father asked, a warm smile playing across his face.

"Um, not really."

Kneeling next to his son, the older man pointed at the

sage-covered bluff on the far side of the water course then to the tree-lined stream and across the grassy bottoms. "Look closer and you can see it. This is a place that is protected from the worst of the weather and a scout on the bluff can see any enemies that might be sneaking up. With good water and grass for horses, it was a fine spot for Indians to camp back years ago."

Now Bill could see it as well. For a moment in his mind he envisioned brush and hide tepees strung out along the willows and trees. A small herd of horses grazing in the lush grass along the stream.

"Yea, I know what you mean," breathed Bill.

"Come on," his father said after a few minutes.

Following his father across the meadow and into the coolness of the shady stream bottom, Bill wondered what his father was going to show him. For several minutes he followed his father as he walked slowly along the banks of the gurgling stream. Then his father knelt and brushed at the ground with his hand.

"Come look at this, Bill."

Stepping next to where his father was, Bill looked at the ground. There, exposed, was a handful of black, glassy flakes of rock.

"Do you know what these are?" his father asked, holding one up for Bill to examine closer.

"Isn't it flint?" Bill asked with awe in his voice.

"That's right. Some people call it flint. But its proper name is obsidian." Then his father explained further. "See how there are quite a few flakes and chips here in this place. Now let me tell you why. See, when an Indian wanted to make an arrowhead, a lance point, or a scraper, he would use an antler point in one hand and piece of buckskin in the other to protect his hand. Then he would flake off the obsidian and make whatever he wanted."

Kneeling next to his father, Bill picked up several of the obsidian chips. "How do you know all of this?"

His father chuckled and picked up several more of the chips. "When I was just a boy, I knew an Indian from up on the reservation. He showed me how it was done."

Feeling as if he was on sacred ground, Bill held the flakes carefully in his palm. "Do you think there are any more?"

"Probably. I've been finding them here ever since I was about your age."

"Have you ever found a real arrowhead?"

"Yes, a couple of times."

His eyes growing larger, Bill asked, "Do you think there are any still here?"

Yawning, Bill's father said, "Well, tell you what. You look around while I take a little rest."

For nearly half an hour Bill searched through the trees and brush. Becoming discouraged, he was about to go back to his father who was napping on the grassy banks of the stream when he was pulled by some unseen force toward a large fallen cottonwood. Plopping down next to it, he began scratching through the stringy slabs of bark and earth with a stick when a glint of black caught his eye. With a forefinger he pushed aside the bit of bark and dirt. An arrowhead! Oh so carefully he picked up the bit of obsidian and held it out. Studying the perfectly shaped piece, Bill wondered for a moment who had made such a thing? What was he like? Then with a burst of excitement he called out to his father.

Two

His brow wrinkled in concentration, the boy known as Bad Foot flaked away a few more minute pieces from the obsidian arrowhead he was working on. Sucking on a finger he had cut a few minutes before, he eyed the arrowhead. Nearly perfect. Using a square of elk hide, he gripped the arrowhead, and with the antler tip of a deer he chipped away a few more pieces of the black stone. There! Putting aside the elk hide he picked out a slender chokecherry limb and with a bit of sinew lashed the new arrowhead to it. Next came three sage hen wing feathers on the opposite end of the limb. The arrow a finished product, Bad Foot slid it into an otter skin quiver alongside six others.

"My son stays busy."

Looking up, Bad Foot saw his father, One Horn.

A grin on his face, the boy held up his quiver of arrows. "Now I have enough to hunt with, or to fight the Crow."

"Aw, a youth of only nine snows can pull a war bow?"

"I can try," replied Bad Foot. Then struggling to his feet, the youth stood proudly before his father holding out a heavy, sinew-backed, wooden bow as well as the quiver of arrows.

With a look of surprise, One Horn took the bow from his son and tested the pull. "It is a strong bow, my son, as good as I have seen. You have been busy."

Beaming with pride, Bad Foot hobbled next to his father and took an arrow from the quiver. "Try it with an arrow."

"Me?" asked One Horn.

"Try it," Bad Foot asked again.

Looking down at his son standing proudly before him, One Horn marveled at this boy. Born with a club foot, his son endured the disability and the difficulty of walking as well as the teasing from other boys that went with it remarkably well. Somehow, One Horn knew his son sensed he would not and never could be like the other young boys of the village. So, at an early age he began to find and develop other skills and talents. Already he had amazed some of the older warriors with his skill at fashioning arrowheads and lance points. And just a week ago, after he had presented his mother with an excellent scraper complete with a wooden handle made from mountain ash, several other women of the village had commissioned him to make them skinning knives or scrapers.

"Should not the maker of such a fine bow be the first to try it?" asked One Horn.

A shy look on his face, Bad Foot replied, "If you wish Father."

Following his son as he hobbled slowly through the stream bottom, One Horn noticed several of the other boys watching with interest. One, Brown Dog, was one of his son's worst tormenters and from the corner of his eye, One Horn noticed the surly boy whisper something to one of the other boys standing nearby.

Downstream, a few minutes of fast walking, was a huge cottonwood tree the boys of the village as well as many of the young warriors used as a target for their bow practice. His son in the lead, One Horn soon became aware they had a following of at least twenty boys and warriors. Then in the rear he noticed half a dozen girls tagging along as well. His mouth set in a grim line, One Horn hoped his son shot straight today.

Stopping at the mark the boys used as a place to shoot their small bows, Bad Foot shook his head. The heavy bow clutched in his hand, he turned and walked back to the spot where the young warriors fired their bows. There he was surprised to see nearly half of the village watching. Such had been his concentration and pride on seeing the look of surprise on his father's face, he hadn't noticed the others following. Swallowing his fear, Bad Foot took the necessary steps back to the farther mark. Taking a deep breath, he fit the last of the arrows he had made to the bow string. As he began to draw the bow he heard the rough sneering voice of Brown Dog.

"The lame one will not be able to draw the bow let alone hit anything with it!"

His lip in his teeth, Bad Foot closed his eyes and thought a quick prayer to his spirit helper, the hawk with the grey wings. Then, with all his concentration on the marked area of the soft cottonwood trunk, he drew back and loosed the arrow. Straight into the black painted circle the arrow flew. For several seconds all was silent. Then from behind him came the trilling war cry.

Turning, Bad Foot saw several of the younger warriors shouting war cries and clapping their hands. Ducking his head, Bad Foot stole a look at his father. Beaming with pride, One Horn was standing next to Owl, the nominal headman of the small village. His chest feeling as if it were about to burst, Bad Foot hobbled to his father and the older warrior.

"The bow shoots well, Father, would you care to shoot it now?"

Grinning from ear to ear, One Horn shook his head, "No, my son. I fear I would look like a novice if I tried to compete with you this day."

Then from somewhere in the back of the crowd came the grumbling voice of Brown Dog. "The lame one must have arrows of magic. I will take a look."

Before the frowning boy could get two steps, Owl held up his hand. "Let the arrow stay! I believe Bad Foot has used skill today. I say let the arrow stay until another can do as well!"

This announcement by the headman caused Brown Dog to duck his head and slink away. Trying not to stare at one of his worst tormenters, Bad Foot turned to Owl and took the remaining six arrows from the otter skin quiver and held them out, "I give these to you as a present."

With a solemn expression, Owl took the offered arrows from the boy. Examining them, he looked up at the crowd and then back to Bad Foot. "These are as fine arrows as I have seen in many years." Then holding the arrows high above his head he called out, "I, Owl, leader of this band give this young man a new name. I give him a new name in honor of his unique skill. I give him the name of The Arrow Maker."

That night in the small village, One Horn gave a feast in honor of his son. As the singing, dancing, and eating began to die down, he walked down to the target. There he was surprised to see his son, sitting, staring at the arrow that remained embedded in the soft wood.

Walking up behind him, One Horn asked, "You are troubled?"

Without taking his eyes from the shaft of the arrow, the boy now known as The Arrow Maker said, "Now Brown Dog really hates me."

"Brown Dog hates what he envies and does not understand. My son, throughout your life you will always meet people like Brown Dog. Whatever they fear, envy, or do not understand they will try to destroy. But do not let yourself be troubled by them. In fact as much as you wish to hate them do not, for they are truly the weak ones. Do not let yourself become as them. Do not become as the striped one who waddles along the ground and smells bad. Remain as your spirit helper and soar on the winds."

For several hours, far into the night, the boy known as The Arrow Maker studied the arrow he had driven into the soft tree and pondered on his father's words.

Three

The sunlight had nearly reached the bottom of the basin now. Shivering slightly in the early morning chill, the old man looked thoughtfully at the partially made lance point. What of the person who had started the blade? Why had he quit? *He probably got pulled aside by something else,* he thought to himself, *just like I did so many times.*

From his light pack, the old man took a water bottle and drank. His eyes going back to the partially made lance point, he wondered what it would be like to try for elk with something like that.

"Pretty hard way to take your winter meat," he said softly to the basin.

The old man's thoughts returned again to earlier years.

The snow crunched under the hooves of the horses as Bill and his father rode through the leafless aspen. Halting his horse for a moment, Bill squinted his eyes against the glare. In front of him, his father stopped his own horse and glanced back. There was a smile on his face as he asked in a whisper, "How are you coming?" Bill nodded a silent reply and urged his horse up beside his father's. They sat side by side for several minutes, the cold air seeping into their legs—father and son sat without speaking or needing to.

After the horses had caught their wind, Bill's father urged his horse toward a shallow pass in the ridge and Bill followed.

Just short of the shallow sagebrush and maple-choked pass, Bill's father stopped. Stiffly, he climbed from his horse and motioned for Bill to do the same. "Why don't we walk over and take a peek? Sometimes the elk will be in the shallow basin on the far side."

With an eager look on his face, Bill tied his horse to a nearby aspen trunk; with fumbling hands, he drew the rifle from the saddle boot. His feet feeling tingly from the cold morning ride, Bill followed his father up and into the pass. Then, one careful step at a time, Bill and his father made their way into the shallow basin. At first, Bill saw nothing. Then his father gripped his arm.

"Do you see them?"

Bill shook his head, his breath catching in his throat with excitement. Then, before his father could point them out, he saw the elk. A dozen cows and calves were bedded down just a mere hundred yards away. A few yards above the cows and calves was a small bull. His heart thumping with excitement,

Bill glanced at his father.

With a knowing grin on his face, his father whispered, "We only need one. You take the shot."

His hands feeling as if they belonged to someone else, Bill remembered the shooting lessons his father had given him.

Kneeling in the snow, he raised the rifle, and, taking a breath, he centered the sights on the bull's shoulder. With a sharp report, the rifle went off, and the bull tried to rear. Then he fell back into the snow. His mouth agape with wonder, Bill didn't even see the cows and calves thunder off in a cloud of powdery snow.

"I got him, Pa!"

"You sure did! Now, let's go take care of him."

Together they walked down through the snow to where the bull lay. Then it hit Bill—he had taken a life.

Seeing the sadness in his son's eyes, Bill's father put his arm around his son's shoulder. "A person feels a little let down right about now."

Going to the magnificent animal, Bill touched the ivory-tipped antlers. "Yeah, I guess I do."

"Do you know why we only killed one?"

"Because that's all we need."

"Exactly. We only kill when there is a reason to do so."

"Some guys don't."

"Just because some people do wrong don't mean we have to do the same," Bill's father replied.

"I know," said Bill, still staring at the fallen elk.

"Come, now," his father said. "We have work to do."

Smiling, Bill rolled up his sleeves and knelt nearby as his father began to dress the animal. Watching with wonder as his father explained the process, Bill wondered if anyone else had ever killed an elk in this spot. Scraping through the snow to make a place for their jackets and rifles, Bill was surprised to see a flash of black stone. Pulling off his glove, he dug around in the wet dirt.

"Pa! Look at this!" Bill exclaimed, holding up a large piece of obsidian.

Pausing his task, his father looked at Bill's find.

"Hey, that looks like a broken lance or spear point."

Taking a closer look at it, Bill's face broke out in a smile. "Looks like I wasn't the only guy to be hunting up here. I wonder if he was as lucky as I was.

"No boy could be so lucky," his father said, a warm look in his eyes.

Four

The early fall sun warming his face, The Arrow Maker and his father studied the small herd of feeding elk. A puff of air on their bronzed faces told The Arrow Maker and One Horn that the breeze was in their favor. For several minutes, father and son watched the twenty or so elk as they cropped the sun-cured grass. Soon winter would come and the elk would need the fat reserves they had built up to survive the bitter cold and deep snows.

Patiently, the pair sat in the cover of a clump of scrubby aspen. With only a slender obsidian-tipped lance, a bow, and quiver of arrows, The Arrow Maker knew he had to be within thirty paces to be able to make a sure kill. His eyes were the only part of him that moved. The youth watched as the herd of elk fed ever closer to his hiding spot. Soon he would have his chance.

In the past week, he had fashioned the sharp blade on the lance. Today, perhaps, his opportunity would come. Over the last year, he had become expert at killing grouse, rabbits, and other small game to supplement the diet of his family. Now, despite his disability, he would get his chance at a larger animal.

Feeling the excitement building within him, he watched as one of the elk, a small bull with spindly antlers, grew closer. Carefully and slowly, The Arrow Maker wiped his sweaty palm on his deerskin leggings. It would be soon.

One Horn watched from several yards behind his son as he prepared to throw the lance. All of the older boys of the small band had already made a kill of the larger animals, and even many of the younger ones had as well. With his lame foot, it was hard for The Arrow Maker to travel very far, and even harder for him to hunt. But now today, with a little luck, his son would take an elk. Soon the band would travel over the divide to the fall buffalo hunting grounds. With a touch of envy, he wished for one of the horses that several warriors of the band had captured. How easy it would be for his son to travel on one of those beasts. For now, when his family moved even short distances, they used dogs to carry the packs, and both of his wives were laden down as well.

Now his son leaned forward. He was ready.

All of his concentration on the young bull elk, The Arrow Maker gripped his lance. Closer the bull fed. Then the bull sensed something! Peering into the thicket of aspen, the young bull ambled a few steps closer. All of its attention riveted on the thicket, the bull seemed to stare into The Arrow

Maker's eyes. For what seemed like an eternity, it stared, trying to make out the two forms crouched in the brush. It then lowered its head and began to feed once more.

With the elk's head hidden by the tall grass, The Arrow Maker's arm shot forward, launching the lance into the chest of the bull. Whirling, the bull raced toward the rest of the elk, who were now milling about. With several sharp barks of alarm, the herd of elk began to run toward the other side of the basin with the stricken bull trailing behind.

His heart pounding in his chest, The Arrow Maker watched the elk as they fled across the sage and grass-covered basin. Then the young bull faltered and sank to the ground. Unable to restrain himself, the boy leaped to his feet and shouted a shrill cry.

Turning with a grin on his face, The Arrow Maker shouted to his father, "I have done it! I have made a kill!"

His bronze face displaying a smile of its own, One Horn nodded. "Yes, you have, my son."

Hopping about on his good foot, the boy called to his father, "Come! We must take it back to the village!"

Following his son as he hobbled across the basin, One Horn's heart was bursting with pride. Surely the spirits were smiling down today.

Coming up on his son as he stood admiring his kill, One Horn put his arm on The Arrow Maker's shoulder. "You have made me proud today, but do not forget, my son, to thank the spirit of the elk for giving us his body."

The Arrow Maker said, "I am sorry, my father."

Ruffling his hair, One Horn spoke to his son. "I believe you will be forgiven. After all, I'm sure the spirit of this elk is honored to be your first kill."

His hand touching the elk's forehead, The Arrow Maker said in a whisper, "Thank you for your body. Your meat will feed many of my people and your skin will keep us warm."

For several heartbeats they said nothing. Then the boy gripped the shaft of the lance and began to work it free. The Arrow Maker looked at the lance head. The point had broken cleanly in half.

"It was a fine point," the boy said.

"Aw, but you will make another," his father said gently.

A smile returned to The Arrow Maker's face and he replied, "Yes, you are right. Come, we need to take the meat home. We will have a feast!"

Five

Again using the antler point, the old man flaked away a few more tiny pieces from the partial lance point. Listening intently, he heard the thin whistle of the bull elk. The old man knew they would be moving into the timber to rest for the day.

Lifting his gaze, he looked to the far side of the basin. There, in the cool fir and pine timber, the elk would spend the heat of the fall day. How many days like this one had he spent here in the mountains? And how many days had he and his wife, Rachel, spent up here?

"Aw, Rachel, I miss ya, gal," the old man whispered softly to the mountain basin.

It was at times like this that his heart ached so. He longed to see her—to touch her and to hear her laughter and see the sparkle in her blue eyes.

His eyes dropping to the obsidian, his thoughts once more went to the past.

Spring! With his heart thumping wildly in his chest, Bill walked quickly along the cottonwood-lined stream planning out in his mind how he was going to ask a girl to the spring dance. The stream was running high with snowmelt and slightly colored. He hadn't had much luck fishing, but then his mind hadn't been on the cutthroat in the stream—it had been on a girl. And not just on any old girl either. Rachel Simms was her name, and in Bill's eyes and mind she was just about the purtiest thing to ever come down the pike. She had long auburn hair and blue eyes that sparkled every time she laughed. The mere sight of her made his knees weak.

With only two days left of school and four until the dance, Bill wondered nervously if he hadn't left asking Rachel for just a bit too long, What if someone else had asked her? But every time in the last week that he had approached Rachel to ask her to the dance, his mind went blank, his mouth went dry, and he couldn't speak a coherent word.

His mind all awhirl, he tromped right past one of his favorite fishing spots. Snapping out of his daydream, he stopped and kicked at a clump of thistle.

"I gotta be crazy or something," he muttered to himself.

Plopping down on a rotted log, Bill began to practice his speech.

"Say there, Rachel, would you care to accompany me to the dance at the high school next Saturday?"

With a shake of his head, Bill rested his bamboo fly rod

on the log beside him. "Nah, that ain't going to work."

Standing, he tried again. "Miss Simms, it would be an honor to escort you to the ball this Saturday. Would you care to accept?"

Kicking at a fallen branch, he shook his head. "How am I gonna do this? Why can't I do it like the other guys and just waltz up to her and say, 'Hey, Rachel, how about going to the dance with me this Saturday?'"

"I don't know? Why can't you?" came a soft voice from behind him.

Whirling, Bill was mortified. Standing behind him, dressed in denim pants and a button-up shirt, stood Rachel! Holding a fishing rod and several trout in one hand, her blue eyes twinkled and the beginnings of a smile hung about her lips.

At first Bill thought he would faint.

"Um," was all he managed to say.

The smile flooding her face, Rachel winked at him and said, "I accept. To all three."

"All three?" Bill managed to croak after he regained the ability to speak.

"Of course. The dance, the ball, and the dance," Rachel said with a giggle.

"Um," Bill managed again.

Laughing, Rachel stepped over the log and took his hand. "I'd love to go to the dance with you."

His eyes nearly bugging out of his sockets, Bill nodded but was unable to make a reply. Fortunately, Rachel took up the conversation. "This is your father's property, isn't it?"

"Uh huh," Bill answered.

"I'm sorry. I should have asked. But my mother really

likes fish and, well, I couldn't help myself. This is the best place for fishing within walking distance, and our car isn't running too well right now."

Finally finding his voice, Bill shrugged his shoulders. "It's okay. Dad doesn't care if a guy . . . or I mean a girl, wants to go fishin'."

Pulling her long hair free of the band that held it in a ponytail, Rachel nodded. "Thank you."

Still feeling embarrassed and somewhat at a loss for words, Bill asked, "Do you really like to fish?"

Her eyes flashing just a bit, Rachel stood back. "Of course. Why?"

Feeling the crimson rush to his face again, Bill held up his hand. "I was just wondering, that's all. Most of the girls I know only want to go fishing with a guy when they are out to impress him . . ."

Realizing he had put his foot in his mouth, boot and all, Bill fell silent, wishing he could find a hole to crawl into.

Then Rachel giggled. "Well, have I impressed you?"

Looking at the four fat trout the girl held up, Bill managed a lopsided grin and nodded. "Yeah."

"Good!" Rachel exclaimed. "But to tell you the truth, I have enjoyed fishing ever since I was a little girl. I used to go with my father all the time."

Bill wanted to ask Rachel about her past and where she had come from. A year ago, when she and her mother had moved to the small town, there had been rumors and gossip, but Bill's father had not been interested in the gossip and had advised Bill to ignore it as well.

"Bill," his father had said. "Don't pay any attention to what folks are saying. Get to know a person before you make any decisions about their character."

"But, Pa . . ." Bill said.

Holding up his hand, his father replied. "Missus Simms and her daughter come to church, don't they?"

"Yes, Pa."

"And they act like decent folks, don't they? And pay their bills? And always have smiles on their faces?"

"Yes, Pa, but folks wonder what happened to Mr. Simms." Bill said.

"Does it really matter?"

Bill shrugged, "No, I reckon it doesn't."

More gently, Bill's father said, "If we needed to know what happened to Mr. Simms, I guess they would tell us. You see, sometimes tragedy strikes a family and it is sometimes easier to move to a different place to make a new start."

In his mind, Bill knew his father was right. Besides Rachel was about the cutest girl around.

"You have done better than I." Bill offered.

A different light in her eyes, Rachel held out a small, metal lure. "Here, try this. It's called a spinner. Daddy always used to use them when the water was murky."

Taking the small lure and tying it to his line, Bill walked with Rachel back to his favorite spot. Within ten minutes he had four fat trout to match Rachel's.

Cutting the spinner from his line, Bill nodded his thanks. "That is some lure. I've heard of them but never used one. They work really well."

"You keep it," Rachel replied with a grin. "You can bring it back when you pick me up Saturday."

Nodding, Bill watched the girl make her way back upstream to the road that led toward town.

What followed was almost like a fairy tale. The dance and many other outings made it seem to Bill as if they were made for each other.

The old man missed Rachel deeply, but soon he knew that he would go to meet her. Flaking a few more chips away from the lance point, he wondered if the man who had begun this had loved another person as deeply as he had loved Rachel.

The Arrow Maker studied the scraper he had made for a woman called Cries At Night. Using some sinew, The Arrow Maker fastened the obsidian blade to a smooth piece of elk horn. There, just right! This one had to be perfect. Four new families had joined the band after the summer festival where many of the different bands of the tribe socialized every year. And this one family in particular had a very interesting daughter, who was of an age when most girls were married. He was also of an age that he should have taken a wife, but not being a warrior and with his disability, he didn't really attract the eyes of the girls in his band. Until now, however, he hadn't really been all that interested in any of the girls. This new girl was different. As of yet, he only knew the girl's name, but he was soon to find out more about her.

At the summer festival, the woman, Cries At Night, had heard of his skill for working with obsidian; after seeing some of his handiwork, she had asked him for a new hide scraper, promising to make it worth his while.

The thought of payment was the furthest thing from his mind as The Arrow Maker hobbled toward the lodge of The Stalker and his wife, Cries At Night. He wondered if their daughter, Sunrise, would be there, or if she would be out gathering wood, picking berries, or performing one of the other tasks that seemed to take up most of a young woman's day.

Stopping in front of the buffalo hide lodge, The Arrow Maker noticed that the sides of the lodge were rolled up to enable the late summer breeze to cool the interior of the lodge. Unable to see anyone, he cleared his throat loudly, hoping to draw someone's attention if they happened to be inside. Then, to his surprise, he saw Sunrise walk around the side of the lodge accompanied by her mother.

For a moment The Arrow Maker's heart stood still. Looking at the slim form of the girl, he knew that she had been aptly named. Unable to speak, he could only stare—wide-eyed and open-mouthed. Catching her eye, he flushed and nearly choked when she smiled coyly at him.

"Aw, I see the young man called The Arrow Maker has called on us," said Cries At Night, breaking the awkward silence.

Stammering, The Arrow Maker held out the combination scraper and skinning knife to Cries At Night. "I brought you the scraper I promised to make for you."

A faint twinkle in her eyes, the older woman took the

scraper and examined it. "It is the finest scraper I have ever seen. How may I return the favor?"

His lips feeling dry, The Arrow Maker shook his head. "It is a gift. A welcoming gift."

Cries At Night raised an eyebrow and said one word that expressed it all: "Ah."

Meeting Sunrise's eyes one more time, The Arrow Maker bobbed his head and turned to go.

"Wait," said Cries At Night. "Will you eat with us?"

With his heart thumping in his chest, The Arrow Maker replied, "I would be honored."

Following Sunrise into the lodge, he took a seat next to the cold fire pit. He did his best to show none of the emotions coming to a boil inside of him.

After several minutes of patient waiting, Sunrise's father and her two younger brothers appeared. Showing no emotion on his face, the older warrior handed a brace of grouse and three large, long-eared rabbits to his wife and settled against his willow backrest next to The Arrow Maker.

The two sat in silence for several more minutes. Then, still showing no emotion, The Stalker said, "It is said you make the best arrows of all our people."

Catching the sly, mischievous grins of Sunrise's two younger brothers, The Arrow Maker replied, "I try my best."

Most young men would have boasted of their ability, and The Arrow Maker's response surprised the older warrior. Before he could make a reply, Cries At Night held out the antler-handled scraper. "The Arrow Maker is too humble. Look at his craftsmanship."

Taking the scraper from his wife, The Stalker examined

the combination knife and scraper with an expert eye. He knew most of the women of the band used tools much more primitive than this. Lifting his gaze to the young man sitting next to him, The Stalker said, "You are too modest. This is as fine a tool as I have seen." Then, knowing his own supply of arrows was getting a little low, he asked, "What would it take for you to make me two hands of arrows?"

"For war or hunting?" asked The Arrow Maker.

The Stalker lifted an eyebrow in surprise and asked, "Does it matter?"

"I believe it does," replied The Arrow Maker. "A war arrow should have a narrower, longer point to penetrate an enemy's shield if necessary. A hunting arrow should be wider."

"I have never heard that." Then, changing the subject, The Stalker motioned with his head toward his wife and daughter as they brought food on slabs of bark. "My wife is a good cook but Sunrise is still learning. Sometimes she makes a mess."

Not knowing if the older warrior was being serious, The Arrow Maker stole a glance at Sunrise and then looked back at her father. He saw a faint glimmer of amusement in The Stalker's eyes.

Finished with the meal of boiled elk, camas cakes, and sage grouse, The Arrow Maker stood to take his leave. "Thank you for the meal. It was excellent." Turning to The Stalker, he said, "I will deliver two hands of hunting arrows in three days."

Watching the young man leave the lodge, Cries At Night mused, "He is a fine craftsman."

"But he will never earn honors in war," answered The Stalker.

"He is an excellent hunter, and the best bow shot in the camp," offered Sunrise, speaking for the first time.

"How is it you know this?" asked The Stalker of his daughter.

Giving her father an unfathomable look, she replied, "There is much you don't know."

With a shake of her long ebony hair, she left the lodge.

For several moments, The Stalker sat silently, wondering what his daughter meant. He looked at his wife and opened his mouth to ask a question, but she silenced him with a wink and a smile.

The old man sat in thought for several moments. How long had it been? Nearly five years had passed since Rachel had gone. He missed her so. Only once before her death had he been separated from her. He remembered that all too well—It was just after he had found the white spear point.

His heart nearly breaking, Bill took Rachel's hand as they walked along the high mountain trail.

"You will come back," Rachel choked out, fighting her own tears.

"Yes, I will," Bill replied.

For several minutes they walked along in silence, the whispering, green aspen leaves giving voice to the mountains.

Stopping, Bill let his eyes wander over the pine and fir-clad ridge above him. He looked down to Rachel, and said, "I have to do this."

Nodding, she put his hand to her cheek. "I know."

"Will you wait for me?"

"You know I will!" Rachel cried with tears streaming down her face.

For what seemed like an eternity, they stood, locked in an embrace, but in the months to come, it would seem like an instant.

Wiping at the wetness on his face, Bill took Rachel's hand and began the long walk down the trail to his father's battered, old truck. Halfway there, he spied a strange, white object lying in the dirt next to the trail. Stooping, Bill pried a long white spear point out of the loose dirt.

"Whom do you suppose made that?" asked Rachel.

"I don't know," Bill answered, turning the point over in his hand. He was intrigued by its color. Over the years he had found several arrowheads and spear points, but they had all been fashioned out of obsidian. This one, however, was made of a hard, white stone not unlike marble.

Handing the lance point to Rachel, Bill wondered out loud, "Do you suppose the feller that made this ever had to go to war?"

"If he did, I just hope it was for the right reasons."

For several heartbeats, Bill was lost in thought. He looked into Rachel's eyes, saying, "You keep this one for me."

"Until you return," she assured him.

Shaking his sore hand, The Arrow Maker looked once more at the white lance point he had been working on. As a challenge to himself, he had attempted to make several arrow points and a lance point from some white, almost transparent stone. And it had been a trial. Not quite flaking like the obsidian, it had proven to be much harder to work with, but now he had five arrows fully fletched with the white points, and he was just finishing the lance head. Engrossed in his work and enjoying the spring sunshine, The Arrow Maker didn't hear the approach of the warriors until they stood next to him. Looking up, he was somewhat disgusted to see his childhood nemesis, Brown Dog, along with a dozen other young warriors.

A sneer on his face, Brown Dog said, "Most of the warriors are going on a raid against the Ute. Are you going to stay in camp with the women?"

Knowing that the young warrior was only trying to make him angry, The Arrow Maker began fitting the white lance point to a slender pine pole.

Seeing his jibe didn't get a reaction from The Arrow Maker, Brown Dog sneered as he stalked away. "The girl, Sunrise, is not interested in a stay behind. She will only have eyes for a warrior."

His heart growing cold at Brown Dog's words, The Arrow Maker's hands stopped their work for a moment. Was it true? Sunrise had been somewhat standoffish in the last while. It probably was true. After all, what kind of girl would want a man who had no honors in war? Or a man without a horse for that matter. Now most of the warriors had at least one horse. The only way to get one of the coveted animals was in war, or by raiding a Ute or Cheyenne camp. And unfortunately, with his lame leg, a horse seemed an impossible prize.

The wet sinew securely binding the white lance head to

the peeled pine staff, The Arrow Maker watched the younger warriors wander off laughing to themselves.

Then he heard his father's voice behind him, "I am sorry, my son."

His own emotions held in check, The Arrow Maker turned and faced his father. "You have done nothing. Why are you sorry?"

"I am sorry that my son does not have two strong feet to carry him to war or on raids."

Trying a smile, The Arrow Maker replied, "My father, was it not you who told me that to make war with another was only looking for your own grave?"

A grin cracking the old face of One Horn, he nodded. "I have said that."

With his eyes wandering down to the center of the village where the lodge of Sunrise's father was, The Arrow Maker asked quietly, "But how am I supposed to earn respect without any battle honors?"

Standing beside his son, One Horn replied, "The Great Spirit will decide how this will take place. You must be prepared for it when that chance comes."

The words of his father soothed his heart a bit. Still, even though he had a reputation as one of the finest workers of stone in the whole tribe, the youth felt somehow unfulfilled.

Bill felt like he had been shoved into purgatory. When it came time to jump from the aircraft, it was as if he had been dropped down a well. And now it felt like an eternity since he had experienced anything that resembled something normal.

Since the attack on Pearl Harbor, and with the war raging in Europe and the Pacific, he had taken more than six months to weigh the decision of joining the Army. Even though the thoughts of leaving Rachel and his family had nearly torn him apart, he had felt that it was his duty to defend his country. The Bible said, "Thou shalt not kill." But the Bible also had many references to the defense of one's country and loved ones. And now, here he was, somewhere in Normandy.

When joining the Army, he had been offered the chance to join the 101st Airborne Division, with a promotion to corporal. Prior to the invasion of France, the men in his unit had been given briefing after briefing, and the most intensive training he had ever experienced. Now he was finally on the ground, with no idea where he was. With the exception of a few flashes of antiaircraft gun fire, he could have still been in England.

The night was as black as coal, and Bill moved a few yards and came up against a stone wall. Resting for a moment, he pulled a canteen from his belt and took a long drink. Never had water tasted so good. Then gunfire and the crackling of hand grenades startled him. Dropping his canteen, which clanked on the stone fence, Bill dropped to the prone position. The fight seemed to be only three or four hundred yards away, and the red lights of tracers and the flashes of more grenades lit up the night. Then it was over. Should he investigate? If he didn't, was he a coward? More than anything, Bill wanted to stay alive and go home to Rachel. But he knew he had his duty.

Silently, as if stalking a deer, Bill crept along the fence. Every so often he would stop and listen and test the night around him for any sign of danger. After ten minutes of sneaking along the fence, Bill heard the faintest of sounds—like rough cloth being brushed against something. Freezing in place, Bill became one with the night around him. There it was again, followed by a low moan. Was it a trick of the Germans to draw him out, or was it a wounded comrade?

Sweat trickling down his face, Bill ran his tongue over dry lips. Then, from the other side of the fence, came another faint noise—the sound of heavy breathing. Holding his own breath, Bill listened to the sound of someone or something breathing hoarsely—a breath and then another; then the breathing stopped, only to begin again a moment later. Wishing he hadn't come to investigate, Bill felt a cramp beginning to build in his thigh.

A flare burst in the east. Bathed in the weak yellow light, Bill risked a peek over the fence. There in the middle of a field of green wheat were at least ten or twelve uniformed bodies, strewn about in every conceivable position. The men wore both the uniforms of American and German soldiers. In the faint light, Bill glanced at the men and knew what must have happened. In the darkness, two patrols from each side had blundered into each other and, from the looks of it, all of them were killed, or the survivors had fled. Bill noticed the body of a young German soldier draped over the stone wall. Wearing no cap or helmet, and with his arms flung downward, the soldier looked as if he were asleep—except for the black-looking blood that covered the front of his gray-green uniform.

Then the soldier opened his eyes and whispered, "Hilfen mir."

Eight

The war party had been gone for nearly four days now, and with the exception of some of the older men and a handful of the youngest warriors, no one was left to protect the small village from attack. So to offer a little more protection to the village, Owl had directed the people to move the lodges into this mountain valley.

Finished with target practice for the day, The Arrow Maker was making his way back to his lodge when a soft voice stopped him. "Mother enjoys the scraper you made for her."

Turning, The Arrow Maker saw Sunrise standing at the edge of the thick stand of aspen that bordered the village.

"I am glad she likes it," The Arrow Maker replied, his eyes drinking in the sight of the girl standing in front of him.

Running his tongue around the inside of his mouth and trying to compose himself, The Arrow Maker held out the lance he had made with the white stone point. "This is my latest creation."

Her finger touching the white point, Sunrise looked closely at it. "I have never seen anything like this. Was it hard to do?"

Grinning and nodding his head, The Arrow Maker replied, "It was very hard." Swinging his quiver from his back, he pulled out an arrow. "I have made five arrows with the same points also."

For several heartbeats, Sunrise studied the points. "You have a gift," she said.

"But I also have this," The Arrow Maker added, holding out his crippled foot.

A scowl crossing her face, Sunrise retorted, "One must not dwell on the things one cannot change." Then she turned and walked away.

His heart feeling as if it had been frozen, The Arrow Maker knew he had hurt Sunrise's feelings. Angry with himself, he trudged back toward his lodge when Owl and another of the older men appeared on the path and stopped him.

"Have you seen Brown Dog and his companions?"

"I have not," replied The Arrow Maker.

"They are supposed to be watching the mouth of the valley, but two women just came back from near there and said they weren't there," Owl stated, an anxious look on his face.

Feeling the need to get away from the village for a while, The Arrow Maker volunteered his services. "I will go to my lodge and get some food, and then I will go there and watch until Brown Dog returns."

His old face turned down in a worried frown, Owl replied, "But you cannot run back with a warning if an enemy is seen."

"But I can shout the war cry," The Arrow Maker returned.

"What he says is true," Owl's companion said. With the frown deepening on his old face, Owl added, "Wait until I find that lazy Brown Dog. He will get a beating."

Knowing most of the village felt that very same way about Brown Dog, with the exception of his own family, The Arrow Maker held his tongue. Heaving a sigh, Owl waved to The Arrow Maker. "Please hurry. I will send another to help you as soon as I can."

Entering his lodge, The Arrow Maker smiled at his mother and his two little sisters. "I have to go to the watching place. Owl says Brown Dog cannot be found and he has asked me to go."

Without a reply, his mother put several strips of dried elk in a leather pouch and handed it to him. Expressing his thanks, The Arrow Maker left the lodge and was making his way to the edge of the village when Sunrise once again stopped him.

"Where are you going?" she asked, her dark eyes expressionless.

With his chest out and a stoic look on his face, he replied, "Owl has asked that I go to the watching place until Brown Dog and his friend can be found."

"Can I go with you?"

Taken by surprise, The Arrow Maker made no reply.

"Please?"

His feelings in turmoil, The Arrow Maker asked, "What

would your mother say?"

"She won't know."

The Arrow Maker wanted to tell Sunrise no, but his heart got in the way. "Will you promise to go back if I tell you to?"

"I promise."

Making his slow way out of the village, The Arrow Maker wanted to make conversation with the lovely girl walking beside him, but his mind and tongue seemed confused and would not work together. Besides, he didn't want to make her angry twice in one day.

"Those aren't our warriors, are they?" Sunrise's voice brought him out of his deep thoughts.

Glancing up, his heart nearly stopped. The thirty or so mounted warriors were not from the village. In fact, they weren't even from the same tribe. They were Cheyenne—the enemy!

His mouth as dry as late summer grass, The Arrow Maker stood rooted, watching the approaching warriors fan out and prepare to attack the defenseless village. Then a low cry from Sunrise unlocked him.

Giving her a shove, he croaked, "Run! Quickly! Spread the alarm."

"But what will you do?" Sunrise asked, her eyes huge with fear.

With a crooked grin of bravado on his face, he pointed at his crippled foot. "I cannot run very fast. I will do what I can."

For a moment, she looked into his eyes. Then she began to run, screaming out a warning to the small village.

With his breath tight in his chest, The Arrow Maker

watched the charging Cheyenne. Somehow he must slow them down. They were mounted and he was on foot with only a slender lance and a quiver of arrows. But if he didn't divert them, his mother and sisters and most of the people in the village would likely perish.

In the failing light of the flare, Bill looked into the eyes of the badly-wounded enemy soldier. What was he saying? Bill didn't speak German, but the look in the man's eyes said it all. He needed help. Bending, Bill brushed his hand over the forehead of the young soldier. "I'll try to help you."

As the flare died and the blackness returned, Bill as gently as possible pulled the young German soldier from the fence. How could he possibly hate this man? But hadn't he in all probability killed Americans just a few minutes ago? His mind filled with questions but no answers, Bill waited in the darkness. Another flare rose into the night sky. In the flickering yellow light, Bill noticed a low stone hut nearly hidden by a thick stand of trees not fifty yards away. After checking for any sign of danger, he knelt and picked up the wounded soldier and carried him to the hut. Now what? His carbine held at the ready, Bill cracked open the door of the hut—nothing but some loose straw. Dragging the moaning German inside, Bill shut the door. Once again the darkness closed in. Now what he needed was light. Searching in the big cargo pockets of his jumpsuit, Bill found the thick stub of a candle that he had been using on the lonely nights while writing letters to Rachel or reading those he had received from her. He lit the wick with a match and placed it on a ledge in the shed. In the weak light of the candle, Bill studied the interior of the low shed. His nose wrinkled. The shed smelled as if it had been used to harbor sheep.

Kneeling near the wounded German, Bill realized that the soldier was a mere boy. Undoing the buttons on the youth's jacket, Bill saw two bullet holes oozing blood. He needed bandages, or something else that could be used to stop the bleeding. Not wanting to venture out into the darkness again, but realizing that he had no choice, Bill whispered a few words of comfort to the wounded soldier and slipped out the door.

The rattle of distant gunfire and the drone of aircraft engines greeted Bill as he crept toward the group of fallen soldiers. One step at a time, Bill worked his way toward the grisly place and soon he touched a body with his foot. Almost recoiling, he stopped and knelt. Reaching out, he could tell from the rough cloth of the uniform the body was not American. With shaking hands, he searched the body of the dead German. Finding nothing that could be used as bandaging, Bill moved to the next soldier and repeated the process. Still he found nothing. After searching over half the dead soldiers, Bill felt sick to his stomach and wanted to run away from this terrible spot, but he knew that if he did, the soldier in the shed would die. Silently, Bill crept to the next form lying over a pile of logs. Using his hands to search the body, Bill's persistence paid off. The dead man was an American medic. With his combat knife, Bill cut the bulky first aid bag containing bandages and other medical supplies free from the dead medic and, with a whispered "thank you," he began to retrace his steps. Then he heard the faint word, "Help."

Freezing in place, Bill's eyes searched the surrounding darkness.

Once again the voice came. "Please help me."

Was it a trick by the Germans? In training he had heard

that the Germans would use all kinds of ruses to trick allied soldiers to come to the aid of a wounded comrade and then kill them.

Taking another step and crouching down, Bill whispered, "Who are you?"

For a while, all Bill could hear was hoarse breathing. Then the soldier spoke. "Name's Neely. I'm hit bad. Can you help me?"

Bill recognized the voice at once—it was a soldier from his own unit named Miller Neely. Somewhat of a bully and disliked by most of the men in his platoon, Private Neely had boasted that he would kill a hundred Germans before the war was over. He had tried to give Bill a hard time, but moved onto greener pastures when Bill had ignored him.

"Please," came Neely's voice once more.

The enemy warriors thundered closer. Already the shouts of alarm were spreading through the village behind him, but he had to give the few men in the village a little more time. With his feet spread wide, The Arrow Maker stood his ground in the middle of the sagebrush covered entrance to the small, mountain valley. Dropping the lance, he put an arrow on the string of his bow. Letting the nearest warrior gallop closer, The Arrow Maker, all in one motion, drew and fired an arrow. Before seeing the effect of the first, he fired a second. The Cheyenne warrior managed to dodge the first arrow but the second struck him in the chest. For several strides of his horse, the mortally stricken warrior tugged at the arrow before sliding from his running mount. A sick feeling came to The Arrow Maker from seeing that he had killed another human being, but he tried to put the thought of his deed from his mind as he faced the rest of the oncoming horde. Firing three more arrows as quickly as possible, he struck another Cheyenne in the arm and another in the thigh, causing the enemy warriors to pull their horses around. Shouting war cries at The Arrow Maker, the Cheyenne retreated just out of arrow range. With his breath coming in great gasps, The Arrow Maker looked toward the fallen warrior, whose horse was standing near him. Retrieving his lance from the ground, The Arrow Maker hobbled over to the dead Cheyenne and cut the rawhide rope that bound the horse to its now dead owner.

Thinking The Arrow Maker was going to scalp or otherwise mutilate their fallen companion, the rest of the Cheyenne charged once more. Tying the lead rope of the nervous war horse around his own waist, The Arrow Maker waited for the charging warriors to grow closer. Once more he fired arrow after arrow at the howling Cheyenne. And once again they retreated, leaving behind another dead warrior and two more who had been struck and wounded with arrows. Then The Arrow Maker's mouth went dry and fear struck his heart. While he had been holding off the Cheyenne at this end of the village, another group of the enemy had found their way to the other end and were now attacking. Hearing the shouts and cries coming from the far side of the village, The Arrow Maker hobbled to the nervous war horse he had captured and mounted. Never before had he sat on one of the beasts, but now he needed the mobility the horse would give him. Tugging on the rope that was attached to the rawhide halter, he rode at a gallop to the far end of the camp.

Thundering into the camp, The Arrow Maker was nearly paralyzed with fear at what he saw. Old men, women, and children lay sprawled about along with several Cheyenne. He noticed a small knot of his people backed up against the aspen thicket fighting the Cheyenne with whatever they could find. Seeing Sunrise fending off a burly enemy warrior with a stout club, The Arrow Maker shouted a war cry of his own and charged his horse at the warrior and Sunrise. Galloping up behind the Cheyenne, thrusting his lance in the back of the enemy, and wrenching the lance free, The Arrow Maker was as a whirlwind. Fighting as if possessed, he soon terrified the remainder of the Cheyenne.

Nearly as quickly as it had begun, the fight was over. Covered with sweat, dust, and the blood of his enemies, The Arrow Maker could only stare in disbelief at the destruction before him. Half of the lodges had been knocked down and bodies lay strewn about. The wailing of the women and children and the cries of the wounded assaulted his ears, causing him to want to cover them with his hands. Slipping to the ground, The Arrow Maker nearly collapsed with fatigue. Then he felt a hand on his arm. It was Sunrise.

Her eyes huge were and dark, and she had a bloody scratch on her face. "Are you all right?" she asked The Arrow Maker

Unable to reply, he only nodded.

"You are a true warrior," said Owl, who had hobbled up. He had a slash on his shoulder and was carrying a broken lance that he used as a staff.

His gaze going to the headman of the village, The Arrow Maker still said nothing.

A woman shouted that he was the savior of the village. Then another and another took up the cry. Soon he was surrounded by the surviving people of the village who were shouting praises to him.

Looking at the desolation before him, The Arrow Maker only felt sick and sad.

Then his mother stood next to him. "What you have done was necessary, my son. If you hadn't fought so bravely, we all may have perished."

Nodding his head, The Arrow Maker wondered if he could ever feel the same as before. By taking another man's life, would he be somehow changed forever?

Nine

The warm sun on his face, the old man thought back to that long night in France. It was so long ago, and yet, at times, it seemed like just a few days past. The darkness, the fear, and caring for the two wounded men. Neely had been shot in both legs and the young German in the chest, but somehow he had, through the long night and the next day, kept the two of them alive.

Swatting at a fly that had somehow survived the fall frosts, the old man chuckled, thinking of the days following the invasion. In the evening on the day after the invasion, he had been joined by three more American paratroopers—two from his own division and one from the 82nd, and a German doctor who just wanted to quit the war and go back to Hanover and deliver babies instead of work on wounded soldiers. The doctor's idea had sounded just fine to all of the men hidden in the stone shed. In fact, the paratrooper from the 82nd had wondered out loud if was possible to wait out the war in the shed. In the days following, the Americans had pushed forward off the beaches and, as Neely put it, caught up to them.

The rest of the war was a blur to the old man. Even the horror of Bastogne and the winter fighting was hard, at times, to recall. But those first two nights were as clear as day—just like the day he came home.

Feeling the train slow, Bill looked out the window for about the hundredth time. Standing, he straightened his uniform and wiped the thin coat of dust from his shiny, paratrooper boots.

"What's her name?" This question came from the sailor who had been with him on the ride north.

"Rachel," Bill replied with a nervous grin.

"She really waited for you all this time?"

"Yup."

"That's something," the sailor replied. "You two must really have something special."

Bill took his duffle bag down from the overhead compartment. Stiffly, he pulled it over his shoulder.

"You still feel it?" the sailor asked, helping Bill get the strap situated.

"Yeah, a little," was the soft reply.

"Did it hurt much?"

"Not at the time," Bill replied. "I didn't even realize I had been hit."

"What was it?" the sailor asked.

"Shrapnel. From a German 88."

"And on the last day of the war?"

Chuckling, Bill nodded. "Yeah, ain't that something? All the way from Normandy and on the last day, boom!"

Shaking his head and grinning, the sailor glanced out the window of the coach. "I'd say." Winking at Bill, he nodded out the window. "Now that is something."

Looking out the window as the train came to a stop, Bill saw what the sailor was talking about. It was Rachel, dressed in a green sweater and skirt, her long auburn hair shining in the sunlight. He had never seen anything so beautiful in his life. Through the window, their eyes met.

For what seemed like an eternity, they looked into each other's souls.

"Hey, you gonna get off?" said the sailor, breaking the spell.

"What's that?" Bill asked, coming out of the trance he had been in.

Laughing, the sailor replied, "If you don't get off this train, I will."

Grinning sheepishly, Bill slapped the sailor on the shoulder and, with a "good luck", hurried from the coach.

Dropping down next to the train, Bill let the duffle bag fall to the ground. Then Rachel was in his arms.

"I've missed you so," she cried as she squeezed him with all her might.

Fumbling with the words, Bill said, "I've missed you too." Then, wincing with pain, he lifted an arm and brushed at a tear that ran down her cheek. "Don't cry. Please, don't cry."

Stepping back and gripping his arms, she asked, "What's wrong? Does it still hurt? Is it your shoulder?"

"I'm fine," Bill replied, drinking in the sight of her. "Really, it's nothing."

Her eyes narrowing, she touched his shoulder with a gentle hand. "You didn't say anything about it still hurting. What happened? Did you reopen the wound?"

"No. Like I said before in my letters, it is just a scratch," Bill answered, pulling her close. "I'm home now. Isn't that more important?"

"Yes," Rachel whispered, nestling herself into his embrace. "Yes."

What followed, the old man realized, was the beginning of a wonderful life. Absently looking at the obsidian in his hand, he wondered once more about the person who had begun the project.

A week following the attack on the village, the war party returned to find that the stature of the young man called The Arrow Maker had increased tenfold.

Now the owner of three horses and with a reputation as a fierce fighter, The Arrow Maker endured the glances cast toward him by the warriors. Standing aside while Owl and another of the old men told the story of his defense of the village, he knew that they were adding to the heroic stand. When Owl came to the part where The Arrow Maker galloped into the camp on the captured war horse, Owl made it sound as if he had killed a hundred of the raiders. But his mind was on other things, namely a young girl called Sunrise.

Waiting until Owl had filled the empty-handed war party in on the battle that saved the village, The Arrow Maker caught the eye of Sunrise as she stood next to her father, The Stalker, who was one of the warriors who had just returned. With a short nod to his own father, who had also been gone with the war party, The Arrow Maker took the halter rope of one of the horses he had captured and walked slowly to where The Stalker and Sunrise stood.

Holding out the rope of the horse, The Arrow Maker asked, "Stalker, I ask for your daughter Sunrise as my wife, and I give you this Cheyenne war horse as a present."

With a sly gleam in his eye, The Stalker asked with a sideways glance at his daughter, "And what does my daughter have to say about this?"

Rocking up on her tiptoes, she smiled and said, "She says yes!"

At her answer, the throng broke out in loud cheering and laughter.

"Then my answer is yes," The Stalker replied gently.

Taking her small hand in his, The Arrow Maker looked into Sunrise's smiling eyes. Lightheaded, he wanted to say something, but once again, the beauty of the girl left him tongue-tied. Finally, he managed to say, "I will try my best to make you happy."

Her eyes shining brightly in the morning sun, Sunrise gave his hand a small squeeze. "I will do my best to make you a good wife."

What followed was, to The Arrow Maker and Sunrise, paradise. Although still hampered somewhat by his club foot, The Arrow Maker did indeed prove to the village that he could provide for a family—a family that he and Sunrise wished for dearly. But three years passed before Sunrise found herself with child.

His face set in a scowl, The Arrow Maker sat on a log in the shade of a huge cottonwood and wished things would hurry. But, as his mother had told him, you don't hurry babies. When they want to come into the world, they will come. Picking up the obsidian knife he was working on, he flaked away several small chips. Unable to control his emotions, he stood and hobbled to the river that was running nearly over its banks from the spring rains and melting winter snows. Bending, he drank and heard someone walking toward him. Whirling, the water dripping from his chin, he saw it was only his father.

"Is it finished?"

His face showing no emotion, One Horn asked, "What is it my son desires?"

With his mouth gaping like a fish taken from the water, The Arrow Maker stuttered, "The baby? It has come?"

"It has."

Straining to hear the sound of a baby's cry coming from the village, The Arrow Maker looked past his father. Then his eyes met his father's and he asked, "I am a father?"

A broad grin covering One Horn's face, he nodded. "You have a son."

Ten

Far off, maybe two or three miles away, the old man heard a rifle shot. Listening, he heard no more.

"Probably got one," he mused to himself.

Turning the obsidian in his hand, he studied it carefully. A little more taken off here and a bit more there and it would be nearly finished. Breathing the mountain air deeply, he absorbed the fall afternoon around him. It was during times like this that he felt lonely. Shifting a little on the sun-warmed rock, the old man let his thoughts run freely.

Bill couldn't stand it anymore. Stopping the tractor, he jumped off the machine and began striding for his house. A few hundred yards from his father's home, Bill had, with

Rachel's guidance, picked the spot and, with the help of a carpenter he knew, built the two-story frame home in a few months.

Married for just two years now, Rachel was expecting their first child. And poor Rachel had had a rough time of it. The last four weeks she had spent in bed with her mother and Bill's mother taking turns watching over her. Last night she had gone into labor. Three weeks earlier than the doctor had hoped, but as Rachel put it, it was time.

On telephoning the doctor, Bill had been told not to move her under any circumstances. Ten minutes later, the doctor had arrived along with a nurse. With a worried look in his eyes, the doctor had shooed him from the house.

All morning he had tended to the farm chores and now, just short of noon, he could stand it no longer. He had to know what was going on and make sure his Rachel was all right. Breaking into a trot as he crossed the newly mown hay, Bill made his way across the field in a few minutes and was going up the gravel drive to his home when his father walked from the front door.

His gaze going past his father and into the house, Bill asked, "Is everything okay?"

"Sit with me," was all his father had to say.

On the porch of his new home was a long, wooden, swinging bench where he and Rachel usually spent the evenings discussing their plans for the future.

Once they reached the bench, Bill's father once more said, "Sit with me."

His heart in his throat, Bill nervously sat down on the edge of the swing. "What's wrong? Is it Rachel?"

His face composed, Bill's father ran his fingers through

his gray hair. "This is a hard thing, son, but you will have to bear it."

Feeling the breath go out of him, Bill listened as his father went on.

"Rachel will probably be all right. But the babies. . . That's right, Rachel had twins—a boy and a girl. Well, the doctor says they just came too early and they only lived for a few minutes."

Feeling a sob well up in his throat, Bill looked at his father. "Can I see Rachel?"

"Just for a moment. She needs her rest."

His body feeling like that of an old man, Bill got to his feet and walked wearily into the house.

Howling with pain, The Arrow Maker's son of six snows, Runner, looked up at the horse he had fallen from. His temper getting the best of him, he beat the ground with his small fists and howled now more from rage than pain.

From his spot on a log, The Arrow Maker shook his head. Never before had he seen a child that was so headstrong and stubborn. He wanted to hobble over and help his son, yet to do so would only make things worse.

The Arrow Maker sat and watched as his young son led the old horse to the rock and once more tried to crawl onto the back of the beast. Once more, the horse let the boy nearly reach its back before it stepped sideways and Runner fell to the ground. This time, however, the boy, in his rage, picked up a stone and plunked the horse in the side, causing it to shy away.

A fierce scowl on his face, the child pulled the rawhide rope that was around the horse's neck until it once more was next to the rock. Then with a flying leap, Runner made it onto the back of the horse. With a satisfied expression on his face, Runner looked to his father for approval.

He gave his son a faint smile in return and nodded his approval. Then the horse shied sideways violently and Runner plopped once more into the sagebrush.

With supper finished, Bill walked outside and made himself comfortable on the porch swing. He was tired, but the harvest was in and he felt good. Feeling a chill in the air, he was about to get up and fetch a jacket from the house when Rachel walked out and put a wool shirt around his shoulders.

"Aren't you cold?"

"A little," he replied as she snuggled against him on the wooden seat of the swing.

As the swing moved back and forth ever so slowly, they said nothing for some time. Watching the early fall sun dip below the western mountains, they generally knew what was on each other's mind.

But not this time.

Rachel spoke up. "I've got something to ask you, Bill."

Moving his head slightly to look at his wife, Bill smiled gently. "Go ahead."

"I have been talking with a lady from the adoption agency. And with some people from the church."

Bill felt a small pang at Rachel's words. It had been seven years since the birth and death of the twins. Since that time, they had wished for more children, but following several visits to several doctors, they had given up any hope of ever having children.

"I see," was all he said.

"What's wrong with adopting a child?" Rachel asked straightening up and staring hard at Bill.

"Nothing," Bill stuttered upon seeing the fire in his wife's eyes. Then, his face turning crimson, he added, "I just never thought about it, that's all."

"But you don't like the idea?"

"Now, I didn't say that," Bill protested.

"But you don't," Rachel accused.

"Woman!" Bill said, his voice filled with exasperation.

"Man!" she shot back.

Heartbeats passed as they looked into each other's eyes.

Finally Bill said, with the ghost of a smile on his lips, "You know, I have always wanted to play Santy Claus."

Kissing him firmly on the lips, Rachel looked into her husband's eyes. "Do you mean that?"

"I do."

"This is your room." Rachel said softly, holding the tiny hand of the little boy.

Standing at the entrance of the upstairs room that Bill had fixed up, Rachel tried her best to communicate with the child, but she was afraid she was failing.

The dark, expressionless eyes of the child stared woodenly at the inside of the colorfully decorated room. Standing behind the small child and Rachel, Bill listened to her talk softly to the boy and wondered what lay in his past. The people from the state adoption agency refused to say much of anything about where the boy had come from or what had happened to him. But from his expressions, or lack of them, Bill knew that his past must have been a nightmare at best.

The boy was an Indian, his name was Evan, and he was just a month more than three years old. That was about all Bill and Rachel knew about the boy. That, and he hadn't said a word since they had begun the drive home.

For several minutes, Rachel knelt and whispered words of kindness to the boy. Awkwardly, Bill stood by and watched. Rachel turned to him.

"Would you mind fixing a bite to eat?"

Nodding his head, Bill retreated down the steps and made his way into the kitchen. Opening two cans of elk stew that Rachel had put up at the cannery earlier in the fall, Bill was about to call out that supper was ready when there was a knock on the front door.

Going to the door, he saw that it was his father, who had been told of the adoption. Stooped and needing a cane to get around, his father still lived alone in his small house just a hundred yards down the county road.

"Thought I'd stop by and see my new grandson," his father said with a grin and a wink.

"And poach a meal too?" Bill replied, a teasing smile on his face. Turning serious, he said, "Dad, I'm going to warn you about this little guy. He looks like some of those kids I saw in Germany at the end of the war."

"Well," his father said heartily. "We can change that, can't we?"

"Yes, we can." It was Rachel, standing at the foot of the stairs, holding the little boy close to her.

For several heartbeats, Bill watched his father as he took in the sight of the child. Then, grinning through his mustache, his father went to the child and, with a grunt, took him from Rachel.

"Say, you look like you could eat. Well, so can I. Now let's see what your new ma has got in the pot."

Eleven

Finished with his sandwich, the old man worked a bit more on the lance point. It would be a thing of rare beauty when it was finished. But now it was still rough. Chuckling to himself, the old man wondered if the man who had begun this had raised any children. And if he did, had it been as rough as making this nearly formed lance point had been, or as challenging as it was raising his own children.

Seeing her eyes as black and cold as the obsidian he worked with, The Arrow Maker wondered what had Sunrise so upset. Stalking into the lodge and beginning to prepare a meal, she said nothing. Wondering if he should ask what was bothering her, his youngest daughter, Paint the Stars, ducked into the lodge followed by her older sister, Catches Rabbits.

"Mother is angry at Runner," Paint the Stars announced.

At eight snows, she was the informer of all that went on in the lodge of The Arrow Maker as well as what was happening in the small village.

"I see," The Arrow Maker replied, watching his wife closely. By her actions, Sunrise was indeed upset with their son. His eyes going back to the job at hand, The Arrow Maker tightened the sinew on the arrow point he was working on.

"She is really angry," Catches Rabbits said following her sister's lead this time.

Her eyes narrowing at her daughter's comments, Sunrise turned on them. "You two sound like old gossips. Now bring in more firewood. It will be cold tonight."

Ducking their heads, the two girls hurried from the lodge.

Putting aside the finished arrow, The Arrow Maker moved next to his wife. Not sure of what to say, he watched a slow tear run down her cheek.

"What has happened?"

Her lip trembling, she replied, "Sometimes our son is so selfish. He thinks only of himself and has no thought of what his actions will bring. He reminds me of Brown Dog."

At Sunrise's last comment, The Arrow Maker had to grit his teeth. Brown Dog, The Arrow Maker's old enemy, had survived the attack on the village many years before, and even though he had been severely reprimanded, he had not changed his ways. In fact, he had become even more loathsome in most of the peoples' eyes. At fifteen snows, Runner was beginning to hang around with Black Stripe, the son of Brown Dog, and a few of the other boys who were, in Sunrise's opinion, not honorable.

His own heart aching, The Arrow Maker stood and awkwardly made his way to the entrance of the lodge. "I will talk with him."

It was nearing evening as The Arrow Maker slowly walked through the village. Here and there people called to him and greeted him with respect. While he wasn't one of the warriors of the village, or even a great hunter, the people respected him for his skill in making arrows, lances, and other useful tools from stone. Some of the fathers even pointed him out to their young sons as a man, who, while he didn't go on raids or war against neighboring tribes, was still a fierce fighter. On the outskirts of the village, he soon found Runner and two other boys.

Catching his son's eye, he motioned for him to come over. Saying something in a low voice to his two friends, Runner stalked over to where his father waited.

With an insolent look on his face, Runner faced his father and asked, "What?"

Keeping his temper in check, The Arrow Maker said in a reasonable voice, "Your mother is crying. Would you like to tell me what happened?"

Unrepentant, Runner shrugged his shoulders. "It is not my fault. She thinks she can run my life and tell me what kind of friends I can have." Then his eyes flashed he thrust his chest out. "I am a warrior. I do not need to listen to an old woman or a crippled man who has few war honors."

Very nearly letting his temper go, The Arrow Maker said nothing for a few moments. He looked closely at his son with hard eyes until Runner dropped his gaze.

"I will not reply to your foolish comments. They do not deserve an answer. You say you are a warrior. You are nothing of the kind."

Turning back toward his lodge, The Arrow Maker added, "Do what you will. But you may not enter your mother's lodge unless you give her the respect she deserves."

Slowly making his way back to his lodge, The Arrow Maker's heart felt as if one of his arrows had penetrated it. What caused a person to be so stubborn, foolish, and selfish?

"Now where has that boy got himself off to?" Rachel said, looking up from placing food on the table.

Glancing at Rachel from the corner of his eye, Bill saw that she had 'the look' on her face once again.

"He's down at the crick," offered Samantha, Bill and Rachel's adopted daughter. She, too, was an Indian, and at twelve years old and three years younger than her brother, she delighted in not only spying on Evan and his friends, but reporting their actions to her mother and father as well.

"And?" Rachel wanted to know.

Smearing huckleberry jelly all over a thick piece of homemade bread, Samantha looked solemnly at her father who was sitting opposite her and said, "I don't think you want to know."

Her hands on her hips, Rachel replied, "Oh, but I do."

Chewing the bread and jelly, Samantha replied, "Are you sure?"

Exasperated, Rachel said, "Yes, I'm sure." Looking at Bill, she added, "Bill?"

Making a "come on" gesture with his hand, Bill said gently, "Sam, you'd better tell us."

"Okay, but it ain't going to be pretty."

"Samantha!" Rachel nearly exploded.

"Okay, Mom," Samantha replied. "Evan and a couple of his friends are down by the big tree smoking."

"Bill!" Rachel's voice cut through him like a knife.

Saying a quiet prayer for guidance, Bill rose from the table, and putting on a light wool jacket, made his way from the house.

With the late afternoon breeze in his face, Bill smelled the tobacco smoke long before he came in sight of the huge cottonwood tree that dominated the creek bottom. Not making any attempt to stay quiet, he walked slowly toward the big tree.

When he was within fifty yards, he heard voices. Then an excited boy's voice said in a loud whisper, "Your dad is coming!"

Bill heard the sounds of several people running away. Stopping for a moment, Bill wondered if he should continue. Lowering his head, he slowly walked to the big tree. Saying nothing, he stood next to the tree for a while until his eye caught the glitter of black on the ground under the old leaves. Stooping, he picked up an arrowhead with the point broken. *Another one,* he thought turning the point over in his hand. *Seems like every time something significant happens in my life I'm finding these,* he mused. The smell of cigarette smoke was still hanging in the air, and Bill knew that Evan wasn't far. Walking to a fallen log, Bill sat and crossed his legs.

In a conversational tone, Bill remarked, "It doesn't do much good to hide."

For several minutes all was still. Finally, from behind a

screen of hawthorne appeared Evan. Evan stood quietly, his dark eyes unfathomable.

With his mind racing, and hoping to say the right thing, Bill looked at the bit of obsidian in his hand. "Who do you think made this?"

For several seconds Evan stood his ground. Then curiosity got the best of him. Coming nearer, he looked at the arrowhead.

Handing the arrowhead to his son, Bill said, "Here."

Turning the point over in his hand, Evan studied the arrowhead for a bit. "I dunno, some Indian probably," he finally said.

"I'd say that was a good guess," Bill replied. "What do you think the Indian was like?" he added.

"Huh?" Evan asked, a surprised look on his face. He was fully expecting to get into an argument with his father, and the way the conversation was going, he was not going to have that opportunity.

"The arrowhead," Bill said. "What do you suppose the man was like who made it?"

"You really get off on this stuff, don't you?" asked Evan, still defiant and wanting the conflict.

With a faint smile on his face, Bill nodded. "Yeah, I guess so. I always wonder what they were like. What their feelings were. How they lived."

"Is that why you adopted me and Sam?" Evan wanted to know.

Shaking his head, Bill answered the question, knowing that his son was trying to start a fight. "No, not at all. You see, after the twins died and your mother couldn't have any more children, we went to the church adoption agency. They are the ones who picked you out for us."

"Why?"

For a moment, Bill said nothing. Then, with the wisp of a smile on his face, Bill said, "Well, it's like this. I always wanted to play Santy Claus."

Evan looked at his father as if he had lost his mind, and shrugged.

"You don't like my reason? Or you don't believe me?"

"I don't know," Evan said absently. The defiant look returned to his face, and he continued, "You know what we were doing?"

"Yes."

"An' you don't care?"

"Sure I care. But if you want to ruin your health, I can't stop you."

"Don't you care about me then?" Evan shot back.

His own smile fading to a grim line, Bill replied, "Evan, you know better than that. But I believe God gave us our own agency to choose between right and wrong. I've seen what happens to people who use tobacco, and I don't want you to end up like that."

Still uncomfortable with his father's comments, Evan said, "Mom send you down here?"

"Not really. I figured we needed to talk."

"Is supper ready?"

"That's why I came down here."

Knowing that his mother may not be as calm as his father was right now, Evan bowed his head. "I'm not hungry."

Taking a deep breath, Bill nodded. "Suit yourself." Getting to his feet, he began to make his way back to the house.

Twelve

It was always in the evening when Sunrise would walk to the edge of the small village and look down the long valley trail that the young warriors had taken. Walking up to stand beside his wife, The Arrow Maker was startled to see a few streaks of gray in her hair. Looking down at one of the otter fur-wrapped braids of his own, he saw some gray there too.

Quietly, he watched as Sunrise shaded her eyes and looked down the trail.

Somehow sensing he was there, she turned to him. "They will return soon."

The Arrow Maker smiled faintly at his wife and nodded. It had been nearly twenty suns since the raiding party had left. And to say that they were looked for was an understatement.

More than twenty-five of the small camp's warriors had gone on the raid. That made up a quarter of the fighting men from the village, and if a war party from another tribe happened along, they would be sorely missed. War parties had gone out from the village all the time, but this time it was different. This time Brown Dog himself had led the party in an effort to gain a little of the prestige he had lost so many years ago. Thus, many of the experienced warriors had refused to go along. It seemed not only to The Arrow Maker but to many of the other older men as well that Brown Dog was a fool, and bad luck. Sadly, many of the younger warriors of only fifteen or so snows had chosen to ride along. And now not only Sunrise but other mothers as well looked for their sons to return.

"They will return," Sunrise said once more.

"Yes," The Arrow Maker replied.

"Perhaps he will have learned something and not be so stubborn," she added.

"Perhaps."

Dressed in a flannel shirt and jeans, Samantha walked out to the small shed behind the house. Opening the door, she ventured inside. There, seated at his work table, Bill held a sharp chisel in his right hand and stared at a large block of maple.

"Hi, Dad."

Turning, Bill grinned at his adopted daughter. Looking back at the block of wood, he touched it with a tentative finger.

"Whatcha makin', Dad?"

"I'm not sure yet," Bill replied.

In the last few years, Bill had become locally famous for

his wood sculptures. Just a few weeks ago, a national magazine had featured him and now he had more work than he could actually handle.

"What do you mean you're not sure yet?" Samantha wanted to know, going to sit next to her father. "Don't you know what you are going to carve when you start?"

"Sometimes," Bill replied. "I have to wait until I feel it here." He touched himself over his heart.

"Kind of like God telling you what to carve?"

"Yeah, something like that," Bill replied with a grin.

"Has he told you what this one will be?"

"No. Not yet," he sighed.

Just then the door to the shed opened. It was Rachel, and tears were streaming down her cheeks.

His heart nearly stopped at seeing the pain in his wife's eyes.

"What's wrong Rachel?" Bill asked.

She tried to speak, and finally the words came: "There's been an accident. It's Evan."

Eyeing a chunk of obsidian that he had partially fashioned into a lance point, The Arrow Maker chipped several more flakes from the point before he heard a scream from the lower end of the village that made the blood in his veins run cold. Grabbing his bow and quiver of arrows, he began to hobble to where the woman was still screaming hysterically.

Because he was slower than most of the other people in the village, The Arrow Maker was one of the last to reach the spot where the woman stood, pointing a finger at an apparition that was staggering up the trail from the lower valley.

For a few minutes, everyone stood rooted as if they were

unable to move. But The Arrow Maker recognized the beaten and bloody form that stood before them. It was one of the younger warriors from the raiding party, and from the looks of things, the young man had been caught by some unseen foe. Naked except for a rude breech cloth, the young warrior had obviously been scalped and whipped within an inch of his life. Somehow, he had escaped his captors and made his way back to the village. The Arrow Maker felt a weight on his arm—it was Sunrise.

With tears flowing down her face, she whispered, "What has happened?"

Wrapping his arm around his wife, The Arrow Maker's heart feeling as cold as if it was made of the obsidian he worked with so often, said ever so softly, "I am afraid our son has left us."

Her shoulders shaking with sobs of grief, Sunrise lowered her head and began to wail.

Tears of his own made their way down his craggy face as The Arrow Maker gently guided his wife back to their lodge.

His heart was filled with fear of the unknown as Bill drove to the county hospital. On the way, they had seen a black car sitting alongside the highway, looking more like a crumpled bit of tin foil than an automobile. On seeing the scene of the accident, Bill had recognized the car at once. It belonged to one of the older high school boys that Evan had started hanging out with.

A state police car was still at the accident scene and Bill slowed, but Rachel choked out, "No, don't stop."

Entering the hospital, Bill's senses were assailed by the

antiseptic smell as well as the sounds of a boy in pain. With Rachel's hand clutched in his, Bill moved swiftly toward the noise but the county sheriff stopped them.

"Bill, you can't go in there," he said gently.

Feeling the pressure of his wife's hand, Bill asked haltingly, "Evan? Is he? I mean . . ."

Pushing his broad brimmed hat back on his head, the sheriff made an attempt to answer Bill's question. "I think your boy will live. One of the others might too. But the rest, well . . ."

Nodding his head, Bill croaked out, "Thanks." Feeling lightheaded with relief, he asked, "What happened?"

"Kids. Racing. I dunno," the sheriff replied, trying to form a reply that made sense to him as well as the parents he would have to face.

Bill could tell that the sheriff wanted to say more—something that would at least give some comfort, but the door to the hospital opened and another set of parents entered. A haunted look came to his eyes, and the sheriff gripped Bill on the arm. "This one ain't gonna be as easy."

Walking slowly, he moved toward the oncoming set of parents as they made their way up the tiled hallway.

Taking a deep breath, Bill guided Rachel over to some chairs set up by the front desk. "Come on, love, let's sit."

Thirteen

The old man leaned back on the rock and watched as the shadows began to creep onto the far side of the small mountain basin. He would have to leave soon. He remembered back to the time of the accident again. Never in his life had he felt such fear, or such relief as when he found out that Evan was going to live. With a grin on his face, he looked at the piece of stone in his hand and remembered the lance point he had finished during that long, agonizing night at the hospital.

Bill looked at his feet. On the polished floor of the hospital waiting room lay a small pile of obsidian chips. With a start, he realized what had happened. While Rachel paced up and down the hall and attempted to comfort the other parents, he had completed a partially made lance point he had found the previous week in a narrow, mountain valley. His mind needing the release, he finished the point with the edge of his pocket knife. Hoping that no one had noticed, he scooped up the flakes and chips and dumped them in a nearby trash can. Glancing at the spear point he had barely finished, he thrust it back into his pocket just as a doctor appeared.

Fatigue showing in his eyes, the doctor motioned to Bill and Rachel to come over.

Before he could say anything, Rachel asked, "Evan? Can we see him? Will he be all right?"

Running a hand over his face, the doctor tried to smile. "Your son will be fine, with one exception."

"What is that?" Rachel asked with a quaver in her voice as she gripped Bill's hand tightly.

His face looking drawn, the doctor said, "Rachel, first I want you to remember this: Two of the four boys didn't come through this accident alive. And from what the police have told me, none of them should have lived. But your son will be fine with one exception—he has lost a foot."

The Arrow Maker touched Sunrise on the cheek. Then, in a smooth motion, he swung into the saddle of his best horse. It was a roan that he had broken as a colt five summers before. The horse not only had the stamina needed for the trip he was undertaking but seemed to know what The Arrow Maker was thinking and would act accordingly.

"You will find our son?" Sunrise asked, her voice subdued and her face drawn.

"I will find him," The Arrow Maker replied.

"You will cover him from the birds and the wolves."

In reply, The Arrow Maker touched his wife tenderly on the cheek and nodded. Then, touching the roan with a heel, he started off.

Armed with his finest bow, a quiver holding two dozen arrows, and a lance, The Arrow Maker had made up his mind that he would find the body of his son and care for it. It might seem to some like a useless and fruitless thing to do, but something in his heart told him to go. And so, three days following the return of the youth, he made up a small pack of food. After telling his wife where he was going, he was off. But what would he find? A few bones now scattered by the wolves and coyotes? Or, possibly, he would find nothing. But still he had to go.

After a week of riding, The Arrow Maker found what he assumed was the site where the war party had met its fate. Knowing that he was in country that was controlled by the enemy tribe the party of warriors had planned on raiding, The Arrow Maker traveled with care.

Hidden in a thicket of aspen, The Arrow Maker studied the sage and willow-lined banks of the small stream that gurgled through the narrow mountain valley. A dead horse lay in view as well as what looked like a body. His stomach knotting up with fear, not for himself but for his son, The Arrow Maker planned his next move.

He waited an hour watching, listening, and testing the air currents. It would be typical of the enemy to watch for members of the tribe to try and recover the dead and then attack them. Knowing that he couldn't move very well on foot, The Arrow Maker urged the roan forward, trusting its senses as well as his own.

It was a body. The animals had been tearing at it, but from the beaded moccasins, he knew it wasn't Runner. Sickened, he had to turn his gaze away. Steeling himself, The Arrow Maker moved on.

Farther up the small valley he saw more signs of the battle—another dead horse and more mutilated bodies. Riding to each one, he took a quick look and kept riding. Reaching the far end of the battle site, The Arrow Maker stopped. Runner was not here. Had he been taken prisoner? He shuddered at that thought. Letting his eyes wander back over the gruesome site once more, his gaze caught on a brush-choked wash that made its way up the side of the mountain. Dismissing the wash, he looked back to the body-strewn battlefield again.

"So, Brown Dog, you have met your end," he said softly.

He made as if to ride off when the wash caught his eye again. It was up the mountain quite a ways and there was no way a person could get there on horse back. But his heart pulled him there.

Turning the roan, The Arrow Maker started up.

An arrow shot's distance from the wash, The Arrow Maker saw a slight smudge on an outcropping of rock. Knowing that this was as far as the roan could take him, he dropped to the ground and examined the smudge. It was dried blood. With his bow gripped in his hand, he studied the way to the wash more carefully now. Here he could see where a person had scrambled up toward the wash and the concealment it offered. Ever so slowly, he made his way up the side of the mountain and soon was at the mouth of the wash. Peering into the brush-choked draw he waited and listened. Someone was in there, and he knew it. Hobbling, he wound his way into the stunted pine and brush. Then a slight sound brought him to a sudden stop. What was that? A faint rasping sounded from just ahead. Silent, even with his club foot, The Arrow Maker crept forward, an arrow on the string of his bow. Soon he was able to make out a form lying on a crude bed of leaves and pine bows.

Another step and the form heard him. Weakly the person struggled to rise and grip an obsidian knife. A knife that The Arrow Maker had made! It was Runner!

Emaciated and looking like a hollow shell of what he had once been, his son looked at him and gasped, "Father!"

Dropping his bow, The Arrow Maker hobbled to his son and took him in his arms. "I am here."

For what seemed like an eternity, father and son wept in silence.

Then, finding his voice, The Arrow Maker asked, "Have you eaten?"

His own voice weak, Runner replied, "Not for some time."

"Come, I have some food on my horse. It is not your mother's cooking, but it will fill you up and give you strength."

With an expectant look on her face, Rachel waited to see how her son would do now that he was fitted with a prosthetic foot.

The door opened and Evan walked out, her husband holding on to her son's shoulder.

"Hey, Mom, how do I look?"

Smiling, Rachel managed a nod—not trusting her voice.

"I like Dad's foot a lot better than that thing the doctor

was trying to get me to wear."

Looking at the white-coated doctor who was standing in the doorway behind Bill and Evan, Rachel saw him wink and smile.

Somewhat awkwardly, Evan thumped over to where his mother stood. Leaning forward, he gave her a fierce hug.

"I love you, Mom," he whispered in her ear.

Standing back, Bill watched Evan and Rachel embrace. Then, in surprise, he watched as Evan held his mother at arm's length. "I'm sorry, Mom. I'm sorry for all of the pain I've caused you and Dad." Wagging a finger at Samantha, he added, "Learn from my mistake, sis."

Grinning back at her brother, Samantha winked and replied, "Don't worry. But things have improved somewhat."

"Oh? How's that?" Evan wanted to know.

"I won't have any trouble outrunning you now when you are trying to catch me."

At this, Evan surprised everyone by laughing. "Yeah, you might right now. But just you wait!"

From his place in the doorway, Bill watched his family. Somehow in answer to his prayers, a miracle had happened. His family was whole once more.

Fourteen

How the children have grown, Bill thought. Evan, despite his artificial foot, had become one of the most respected engineers in his field. And he had three kids of his own. Samantha lived just an hour's drive away with her own family.

Hearing the bugle of the bull elk in the timber on the far side of the basin, Bill looked through his binoculars for the elk. There! They were just vague shapes moving through the timber. Soon they would come out to feed, just like the last time he had taken an elk. It was with fondness he remembered the time. It was the last time he and Rachel had come here together.

"There he is," Rachel whispered.

Straining his eyes, Bill looked but couldn't see anything in the faint light of the predawn sky.

Then came the screaming bugle of the bull elk as he answered Bill's bugle.

"Man, he's close," Bill whispered.

"You'd better get ready," Rachel hissed back.

"I'm always ready," Bill replied in hushed tones.

Then the bull was there, standing not over fifty yards away at the edge of the pine timber. Stretching his neck, the bull screamed out his challenge again. With fury, he began to whip a small pine with his massive rack.

"Bill!" Rachel croaked. "You'd better . . ."

What she was about to say was drowned out by the roar of Bill's rifle. Staggering, the bull slumped to the ground. For several moments, Bill and Rachel stared silently at the majestic form of the bull elk. Then, slowly, they walked to where the bull lay.

"Always kinda gets to you, doesn't it?" Bill said with reverence in his voice.

"Yeah," Rachel replied.

Reaching out, Bill touched the massive rack; in his heart he whispered a silent prayer of thanks. He had always heard that the Indians had given thanks when they made a kill, and how could he do less?

"Grandfather, what are you saying?"

It was his oldest grandson, The Rattler, speaking.

The Arrow Maker turned to the boy of six summers, the son of his daughter Catches Rabbits.

"I am thanking the Great Spirit for giving us this deer for food," The Arrow Maker replied, smiling gently.

"But you killed it with your bow."

"What you say is true, but The Great Spirit created this deer and allowed it to be in this place and guided my arrow to the proper spot."

His face set in a thoughtful expression as he watched his grandfather cut meat from the carcass of the deer, The Rattler thought this over.

"What you say must be true, Grandfather."

Chuckling, The Arrow Maker winked at his grandson, "You are wise for your years. Remember, always let the Great Spirit guide you. Do not let anger or other feelings influence your actions."

"Is that why you have lived so long?"

Suppressing a laugh, The Arrow Maker nodded. "I guess so."

"And that is how you found my uncle The Runner?"

Another nod. "That is true, my grandson."

"He is a great man," The Rattler said absently.

"Yes, he is. And you will be an even greater man if you but follow the whispering of the Great Spirit."

With a solemn expression on his face, The Rattler nodded his head. "I will try my best, Grandfather."

"That is all we can do," The Arrow Maker replied.

Nearly done with dressing the bull, Bill heard someone coming through the brush behind him.

"It's Evan," said Rachel.

Straightening up, Bill massaged the small of his back. A glance told him that it was indeed his son. With a shake of his head, he wondered how Evan managed to get around in the mountains with his disability.

Waving his hand, Evan walked up. "You did it again, didn't you?"

"What do you mean?" Bill asked.

"Got a nice bull." Evan replied with a shake of his head. "I don't know how you do it."

"Aw, just lucky I guess," Bill said. Looking around, he asked, "Say, have you lost my grandsons?"

Chuckling, Evan shook his head. "No. Kurt and Doug decided they were old enough to go by themselves for a bit. They can't get too lost. They are hunting down the main ridge toward the truck."

"You lose my grandsons, and Samantha won't have to kill you—I will," Rachel said eyeing her son.

Looking at his parents, Evan smiled and shook his head.

"Come on, Mom. Remember the time you and dad sent me off down the ridge with Sam the first time?"

"You got lost," Rachel accused.

"Not lost. Just turned around," Evan shot back, his eyes sparkling with amusement.

"Lost," repeated Rachel.

Watching his wife and son as they retold the story for about the thousandth time, Bill took in the view. It was beautiful. The mountains and everything were so perfect. How many more years would they come, though? Rachel's dark hair had turned silver and his own was gray. And now it took him twice the time to make his way here than before.

"Well, if you two are going to argue about something that happened thirty years ago, I'll go get the horses," Bill said to Rachel and Evan.

"Lost," Rachel said with a wink. To Bill she said, "Go ahead. I'll wait here with Evan."

Concerned, Bill asked, "Are you feeling all right?"

With a gentle smile on her face, she replied, "Just fine, old man. But this old woman is a bit tired."

"We'll wait here, Dad," Evan put in. "The elk will be ready to load on the horses when you get back."

Bill waved and started down the trail. "I'll see if I can find those two boys on the way. They'll be good help."

His heart still ached from the loss of his wife, and for a few moments, the old man stared farther down into the basin. It hadn't been but a month after that last trip when suddenly his Rachel was gone—but not really gone. There were times when he could feel her presence—as if she were watching over his shoulder.

Looking at the obsidian in his hand, he wondered if the man who had started the point had been left alone?

Fifteen

"Grandfather?"

Turning slightly to see his grandson, The Rattler, walking up the trail, The Arrow Maker let a small smile steal across his face. It was the first in sometime.

Sitting next to his grandfather, The Rattler offered him a chunk of roasted elk meat on a slab of bark. "It is still warm."

Nodding, The Arrow Maker took the meat and set it near his side.

"Mother worries," offered The Rattler.

"I will be fine," The Arrow Maker said quietly.

For several minutes the two sat in silence.

Finally, The Rattler said, "Grandfather, you need to eat.

Grandmother would not want you to starve to death."

A dry chuckle escaped The Arrow Maker at that. Picking up the elk meat, he nibbled at it. "You are right. She wouldn't like me to die that way."

At seventeen snows, The Rattler sat patiently and watched as his grandfather ate the elk meat. It was just more than three moons since his grandmother had died and still his grandfather grieved. For days on end he would find a spot away from the village and sit by himself. Never in his young life had he seen two people so bonded together. It was like when one of the great white birds lost a mate. It was said that they would even die of loneliness.

He was lost in his own thoughts when his grandfather's voice interrupted him. "What is it you wish to talk about?"

"Aw, Grandfather. I don't know. I have many things on my mind."

Again The Arrow Maker chuckled. "I remember when I was your age."

"My age?"

"Of course. Don't you believe that this wrinkled old body was once like yours?"

With a crooked grin on his face, The Rattler nodded. "Yes, Grandfather. I know that."

"You worry about your future and what lies ahead," The Arrow Maker stated to his grandson.

"Yes," came the reply.

"You are wise beyond your years, my grandson," The Arrow Maker began. "It will take a man like you to lead this people through what lies in the future. Great changes are coming and you can make the difference between a sad end for this people or a future of greatness."

His eyes large, The Rattler stared at his grandfather. "What do you mean?"

"Are you not concerned with the white ones who are coming into our country?"

"Yes."

"Haven't you seen the change that has already come to the people?"

"What do you mean?" The Rattler wanted to know.

A soft smile played at the corners of his mouth as The Arrow Maker went on. "How many of the men come to me for arrows now? Not many. Most of the men now own the guns of the whites. The women want the sharp knives of steel, not the obsidian scrapers I used to make. How many of the women have a metal pot to cook in?" With a chuckle, he answered his own question. "It is a poor husband indeed who has not provided his woman with one. Do you see what I mean?"

With a smile of his own, The Rattler nodded. "What you say is true, my grandfather." Frowning, he added, "But some of the people say the white ones will go away."

"What do you think?"

"No," The Rattler shook his head. "There will be more. Soon they will cover the land."

"That is as I believe," The Arrow Maker said. "And you must learn to live with the white ones and ensure that the people learn how to live with them as well."

With the beginnings of a frown coming to his face, The Rattler said, "But, Grandfather, the whites are different from us. They dig up the earth, and they sometimes lie and steal. And some of them trade our men water that makes them crazy."

"That is true," The Arrow Maker replied. "Some of the

whites are bad people. But remember the story of Brown Dog? Was he not a bad person?"

"Yes, he was," acknowledged The Rattler.

"We are all creations of the Great Spirit," The Arrow Maker said. "Some of us are good and some are bad. Some of us are red and some are white." Touching his grandson on the shoulder he added, "Remember Broken Hair's wife and how she was saved from drowning by a white man?"

With understanding coming into his eyes, The Rattler nodded his head. "Yes, I remember."

Then, a faraway look coming to his face, The Arrow Maker finished. "Soon I will be gone. Soon I will go to meet Sunrise and you will be here to guide the people. Do so wisely, my grandson."

For some time they sat side by side watching the sun begin to dip below the ridge on the far side of the basin.

Getting to his feet, The Rattler brushed at the dust on his buckskin leggings. "We should start back to the village. Mother will be worried."

With a gentle smile on his face, The Arrow Maker nodded. "Go ahead. I will be along in a little while."

Nodding a reply, The Rattler started down the trail toward the small village.

Watching his grandson leave, The Arrow Maker turned the piece of obsidian over in his rough hands. How many times had he worked with the stone to make something useful for his people? But now there wasn't much use for his tools or points. And not much use for him either. He sighed and looked at the far side of the basin. What would happen to his people? Would they survive? Would they still be a proud and prosperous people?

Chipping away a few flakes from the obsidian in his hands, he heard a soft voice from behind him. A chill shot up his spine when he recognized the voice. It was Sunrise!

Dropping the obsidian to the ground, he turned and she stood next to him.

Laughing, she held out her hand. "Come, my love, you have waited long enough."

In an hour it would be dark. The old man chipped away a few more flakes and the point was finished. Turning the finished point over in his rough hands, the old man admired his work. No, not his—someone or something had guided his hands. Just like with his wood sculptures, just like his life. He, as well as Rachel and his family, had started out as rough shapes. By the gentle but firm hands of God, he had been fashioned into something much more polished.

What now, the old man wondered? He had several blocks of wood waiting for him in his shop, including that same old dusty chunk of maple from the time Evan had lost his foot, but no idea of what to carve next.

Well, time to go. If he was to get back to his truck before dark, he would have to leave now. Making a move to get up from his seat, he heard a whisper of clothing. Turning sharply, he was surprised to see a man standing beside him.

Dressed in buckskin, the man had a gentle smile on his face.

"You sure startled me," the old man said with a nervous laugh.

"I'm sorry," the stranger replied, straightening one of the long braids that hung down over his chest.

For several heartbeats, the old man stared into the dark

eyes of the stranger. "I was just leaving," he said. "You need a ride anywhere?"

"No." Nodding at the obsidian point in the old man's hand, the stranger said, "That is a fine job you have done."

With a crooked grin, the old man shrugged his shoulders. "Aw, wasn't nothing. I been fooling with these all my life."

Returning the old man's smile, the stranger said, "I, too, worked with stone."

Again came the awkward silence. Then with sudden clarity, it came to the old man.

"It's time, isn't it?" he asked.

A gentle smile and a nod from the Indian answered his question.

His eyes sweeping the basin, the old man murmured, "Have I done any good?"

"Yes, you have."

"I tried. I really did."

Then all the memories flooded back—the good, and the bad. He remembered the happy times and the tears. "What about the kids?" the old man murmured.

"You have led them down the right path," the stranger said. "For that I am in your debt. They are of my blood."

Nodding, the old man grinned and asked, "The arrowheads, the points—all those were yours?"

"Yes."

Handing the stranger the finished point, the old man said, "I figger this is yours."

With a smile and a nod the Indian was gone and then Rachel was there.

Epilogue

Entering the old house, Evan was immediately flooded with memories. Breathing in, he closed his eyes and recalled the smells, the sights, and the sounds. Opening his eyes, he looked in the corner near the big window. It was there that the Christmas tree was always placed. For a second, he was once again back in his childhood, running down from upstairs with Samantha. He always hoped to be the first to be awake, but somehow his father was always sitting in the rocker waiting. And there always seemed to be wonderful smells coming from the kitchen where his mother reigned.

Absently, Evan wandered from room to room searching for something but not knowing what. After a half hour, he found himself walking out the back door and entering the small wooden building where his father did his woodwork. Opening the door, he stepped inside. At once the smells of pine, oak, and other woods came to him.

They were both gone now, and inside he felt lost. Even though Bill and Rachel weren't his real parents, Evan still felt a deep love and a strange loss. Moving slowly around the shop, Evan took in the smells and the memories. It was here that he had gained an education more valuable than his degrees from three different universities—an education in life.

Then his eyes caught a dusty chunk of maple that sat on a corner shelf. Thumping over to it, he picked it up. This was the one his father was going to start on the day Evan lost his foot in the accident that changed his life. Many times since, Evan knew his father had wanted to carve something from this particular piece of wood but nothing would come. Or, as his father had always said, the wood hadn't told him what it wanted to be.

A true craftsman, his father always believed that each piece of wood would tell him what he should carve from it.

Picking up the maple, Evan walked with it to the workbench and locked it in the vise. Plopping down on his father's old stool, he stared at the wood. In the last few years, he had picked up the woodcarving habit as a way to bleed off some of the stress of the life that he and his family had been living.

Hearing a faint noise, Evan turned to see his wife, Sheri. She was dressed differently than usual, in a flannel shirt with the sleeves rolled up and jeans. She reminded him of his mother.

"Hey," he said softly.

Walking up, she put her hands on Evan's shoulders. "Do you need some time?"

"No," he replied. "Just sittin' here thinking." Glancing back at his wife, Evan chuckled.

"What is it?" Sheri wanted to know.

"You sure look different."

"What do you mean?" she asked, raising an eyebrow.

"Your friends in L.A. wouldn't know you."

A short laugh and Sheri shook her loose blonde hair. "Oh, well." Then with a faraway look in her eyes she said, "Evan, I don't want to go back."

Reaching up, he took her hand. "Neither do I."

For several moments they sat in silence, before Evan took a black object from his pocket.

"What's that?" Sheri wanted to know.

"They found it with Dad. It's another spear or arrow point. You know how he was always making them or finding them."

"Just another arrow point?" Sheri asked.

"No, not just another one," Evan replied. Looking back at the block of maple, he could see what lay inside the wood. Tentatively, he picked up one of the sharp chisels and scraped at the surface of the wood.

"What is it, Evan?"

His voice catching, Evan answered his wife. "I know what this piece of wood is supposed to be."

Knowing that Evan had started carving in his spare time, Sheri asked again, "What is it?"

In his mind, Evan could see an old man dressed in buckskin. The old man worked at chipping an arrowhead from obsidian.

In silence, Sheri watched as her husband began with sure smooth strokes to carve the wood.

Down by the cottonwood-lined stream a young, dark-haired boy and a younger girl were exploring. With a gasp of amazement, the boy spied something. Digging through the debris on the ground, the boy soon held an obsidian lance point.

"Look, sis. Looky at what I found," He whispered in a reverent voice.

Crouched beside her brother, she peered over his shoulder. "Maybe the stories dad tells us are true."

Straightening, the boy looked out over the stream bottoms and in his mind he could see buffalo hide and brush lodges strung up and down the stream. A herd of horses grazed on the lush grass and leather clad figures went about their tasks.

"Yeah, they are."

About the Author

David J Hawkes was born in a small community in Idaho. He attended Ricks College and served a mission for the LDS Church in Italy.

David enjoys community service and working with young people, teaching them responsibility and values. He also enjoys the outdoors and has spent much of his life working for the Idaho Fish and Game Department. He has served in the Army National Guard and currently works for the U.S. Forest Service.

He loves history and has experienced much of what he writes about. *Obsidian* is his fourth book.

David and his wife, Susan, live in Franklin, Idaho, with their two daughters.

To learn more about David's books, e-mail him at hawkpublishing@aol.com.